THE WRITERS CIRCLE

Edited By:
Nathan Primeau
Abigail Rabishaw

PRIME
PRESS

Prime Press
contact@primepress.ca
www.primepress.ca

ISBN 978-0-99366-510-3 (perfect bound)

The Writers Circle Logo by Nathan Primeau
Prime Press Logo by Zak Hartong
Book Cover by Nathan Primeau
Book Design by Nathan Primeau
Printed in the United States of America

First Edition

14 13 12 11 10 / 10 9 8 7 6 5 4 3 2 1

COPYRIGHTS

CONTENTS

FICTION

POETRY

NONFICTION

WHAT IS TWC?

The Writers Circle (TWC) is a community of writers that communicate with each other through social networks.

The Writers Circle anthology has collected a series of stories and poems from The Writers Circle community and open submissions.

The selected entries exhibit various depictions of "beginnings". The freedom as to which sort of beginnings are presented within each contribution is at the discretion of the writers.

FICTION

RUNNING TO THE FOREST
MARY SWORD

This is the only way to get away. She knows that.

That didn't mean it was going to be easy, though.

She sighed, looking down at the infant clutched to her chest.

He is going to be such a good man one day. She's sure of it. It's one of the only things she was sure of; her son is going to be a good man, and she isn't going to let anything stand in the way of him getting the chance to become that man. Especially not Caleb.

It's the only way. Michael needs to chance to live; he won't get that chance here.

She clutched at her head with her free hand, the handle of the cold knife knocked into her as she raked her fingernails through her scalp. She shook her head roughly, trying to clear her mind.

This is the only way. This is the only way that her and Michael are going to get any chance at a real life. This is the only way they'll be able to start over.

If she didn't do this then it would just be more of the same routine; they'd run and a week later there would be a banging on the door and in would barge Caleb, dripping with sweat, screaming and swearing and throwing punches all over the place.

It didn't matter to him that she didn't want anything to do with him.

It didn't matter to him that Michael needed medicine.

It didn't matter to him that she had bruises and scars covering her body.

It didn't matter to him that they just wanted to leave.

It didn't matter to him that they wanted nothing to do with him.

They were his; they belonged to him.

Nothing matters except him, don't you know?

She laughed. It was a hallow chuckle. Nothing was funny. At the same time, though, everything was funny. This whole situation was ridiculous.

She is holding a knife.

She is going to stab her husband.

She is going to take her son and run and never think about him or this cabin ever again.

And isn't that just fucking hilarious?

She gripped the knife tighter in her hand and shifted Michael in her arms so that he's facing her chest now. He isn't going to see what's about to happen.

Looking around the room, she took in what had been her home for so long one last time.

The kitchen she stood in was dingy, dirt and dust covering every inch of the room. The light shone through the curtain-less windows, a beautiful forest waiting just a few steps from the cabin front doors. This is the forest that they are going to escape into. In this forest she was going to run until she couldn't run anymore. Eventually she'd find help; but she'd get as far away from this cabin as she could first.

On the kitchen table she'd left a letter, written as neatly as was possible with her shaking hands, explaining to whoever happened to stumble upon the cabin and Caleb what had happened. It didn't matter though; no one was going to find this cabin for a long time. Caleb had made sure it had been out where no one would ever go.

The government is always watching, babe. We've got to keep away from them.

She turned her head toward the hallway in front of her. It led to the room where she was going to do it; where Caleb was sleeping in his recliner.

Slowly, she walked through the dusty hallway, clutching Michael even tighter to her chest as she went. She needed to be silent. She needed to do this. This is the only way. The world will be better off without him. Michael is going to be a good man. She would be a good mother and they were going to have a better life.

She just needed to get them away from Caleb. Once they were away from him then everything would be alright. Michael would get the life he deserved.

She stood over Caleb as he slept, watching him dream silently. The hand that held the knife in it had started to feel numb.

She's screaming at herself inside her own head; screaming to just get the job done so that they could run away into the forest.

She raised the knife above her hand, hovering it over Caleb's chest.

Do it.

This is the only way.

Do it.

Michael will be such a good man.

Michael will be better than Caleb.

Do it.

Blood spattered on her and Michael as she quickly sliced through Caleb's throat.

His eyes jerked open, mouth agape as he stared at her while

he clutched the pulsating wound in his neck; but it was too late – she'd cut too deep and too quick for him to do anything more than flail around wildly.

She stepped back and watched him for a moment, and then buried her face into Michael's blankets.

She stood there silently for a moment, not really believing she had done it. She could hear as Caleb gasped for breath; could hear the life leaving his body in front of her.

She'd done it.

She'd killed a man.

She'd killed Caleb.

She stayed with her face buried for a few more moments, listening until Caleb and the house were silent again.

Blood was all over the floor; Caleb had fallen back against the recliner, his hands were still clutched at his red and gushing throat. As she stared at the wound under his dead hands it hit her.

She'd done it.

She was free.

She felt a rush throughout her body as she ran to the front door and had slammed it open with her free hand. The outside air lifted the dust in the musty cabin with a welcome freshness. The wind felt cold against the blood splattered on her face; but it was a nice cold, it was a reminder that she was free.

She stepped out and felt the hard ground under her feet.

She was free.

She ran towards the forest. She didn't know what the future was going to bring; she didn't know how they were going to make this new life for themselves or how far she was going to get into the forest before she had to find help or how she was going to explain the blood covering her and her son; but she was free of Caleb, and that was enough for her in that moment.

CLIMBING
TERRY SANVILLE

1.

Brian pressed his cheek against the trunk's rough bark. It smelled like butterscotch. He felt the pine tremble in the wind. The branch that he clutched with his legs thrashed about. He had no idea how he'd got there. One moment he'd been spinning his lovely wife across a Vegas dance floor and the next he was gripping the tree. The sleeves of his sports coat rode up to reveal the Rolex she'd given him for their silver anniversary. The watch had stopped.

He stared downward. A swirling greenish-gray mist hid everything. The tree trunk disappeared into the fog with no branches to climb down on. He fumbled in his pocket for something to drop, to determine if the ground might be close. Grabbing his hard-shell glasses case, he filled it with pocket change, shut it tight, and then released it. He held his breath and listened. Only the moaning wind made any sound. He turned on his smart phone, no bars. Brian stared upward at blue sky and sunlit limbs. Maybe my phone will work if I climb higher, he thought, and pushed himself up, his leather-soled shoes slipping on the branch's rounded surface.

The tree limbs above him ascended like a giant spoked ladder.

With unsteady legs he started climbing. The scented air burned his lungs.

2.

As Brian moved upward, shafts of sunlight showed his tree to be one of many in a forest of indeterminate size. Other sounds now echoed through the woods: the screech of hawks, the chatter of squirrels, the complaints of Steller's jays. He moved slowly, carefully, remembering to keep a three-point contact with the tree. Black spots danced before his eyes and he sat on a limb to catch his breath. He stared outward along the branch. Maybe fifteen feet from the trunk, someone had built a platform that spanned the space between two limbs. A crude wooden hut clung to the planks. A boy sat in its open door, his head bowed, as if sleeping.

"Hey, are you okay?" Brian called.

The boy raised his head and grinned. "Better than you."

"What are you doing here?"

"What does it look like? I'm building a tree house – like the one you and Steve built but wouldn't let me help."

"Who are you?"

"Don't you recognize me? I'm Larry, lived down the block from you. We went to the same school."

"Right, Larry…Larry Conklin. But that was almost forty year ago. How can you still be a child?"

"That's for me to know and you to find out. You will, soon."

"What's that supposed to mean?"

"You never let me play with you even when I begged you to. Why were you so mean to me?"

"I…I didn't mean to be mean. You were younger. You know how kids are; the older ones won't play with the little ones."

"But you really hurt me. I never forgot."

"I'm sorry."

"Yeah, well now you're too old to do young things. How does it feel? That's how I felt back then. And for no reason."

"You're right, you're right. But what can I do now?"

"Nothing. Just keep climbing. There's more." Larry stood and moved inside the hut and closed its door. The light dimmed, as if the sun went behind a cloud. Brian stared upward. A cold chill ran through him. He rose and climbed on.

3.

A sunlight shaft warmed Brian's shoulders and he stopped to check his cellphone; still no service. He breathed in, out, in, out, as if that simple function had more importance now. Below, the mist had risen to meet him. He reached upward to grab the next branch and continue his ascent. But a voice called to him from out of the fog.

"Wait, wait, don't go just yet."

He slumped onto the branch, his whole body trembling. A young woman with milky-white skin and hair the color of outer space climbed toward him. She wore a revealing dress, her bare feet expertly moving from branch to branch. With strong arms she pulled herself up and sat on the limb next to him. He stared at her face with its high cheeks, dark eyes, and pouting lips. Sliding an arm around his waist, she clutched him tightly and kissed him. His heart pounded and so did hers.

"Where have you been?" she asked. "You never called. And that last night we had was so fantastic."

"I'm…I'm sorry, but do I know you?"

She smiled. "Of course you do. I'm a friend from high school."

"Yes, yes, now I remember. I had you in Spanish Class."

She chuckled. "You had me in the back seat of your car, after the senior party."

"Oh, God, it really is you. You're…you're…"

"Sandra, and you don't need to be embarrassed. Actually, you should be."

"You're right, I should be. What happened to you?"

"What happened to me?" The girl frowned and stared downward into the mist. "You never called. I was afraid you'd be one of those 'love 'em and leave 'em' guys. I was right, wasn't I?"

"I was a punk back then. We all did hurtful things."

"Yeah, well you went off to college and I went off to a home for unwed mothers."

"You had a child?"

"He was the love of my life. But without a father he ran with the wrong crowd. Some gang bangers shot up our place. He didn't make it. It destroyed me."

"Christ...I didn't know. Why didn't you tell..."

"Just shut up. All you had to do was pick up the phone."

Sandra pulled away and climbed out to the end of their limb until it bowed downward. She blew him a kiss and slipped from the branch, spinning slowly like a dandelion seed, and disappeared into the mist. Brian stared wide-eyed then touched his lips. He savored the lingering taste from her kiss. Memories of that forgotten night came flooding back, the torture of young love, the panic to undress, the press of bare flesh. They made his chest ache even worse.

Brian shook himself, pulled his jacket shut and climbed on.

4.

He struggled to breathe. The chest pain grew intense. The wind died and the air felt hot, desert hot but scented with evergreens. Sweat trickled between his eyes and dripped from his nose. His feet hurt but he continued upward, checking his phone often for service. Above him, a hulking form leaned against the trunk. He stopped, thinking it might be a wayward bear scared into the treetop. What a stupid way to go, he thought. Being mauled by Smokey with no place to run.

But the shape remained motionless. Brian edged upward. What had looked like a twig or branch extending out from the trunk resolved into an M16 rifle and the shape into a soldier dressed in desert fatigues. As he climbed nearer, the man called to him.

"What are my orders, Sergeant? What are my orders?"

"Stand down, soldier." The words came to Brian's lips without even thinking, though he hadn't used them in more than twenty-five years.

The soldier leaned back against the trunk, his rifle pointed skyward. "Have you brought a replacement, Sarge?"

"No, it's just me."

Brian had climbed onto a limb below and off to one side of the soldier. He craned his neck to stare upward, noting the black PFC pins on the collar of the man's camouflage uniform.

"How goes the watch, private?"

"Can't see nothin', Sarge. Black as hell out there, and the wind makes me hear things."

"Hear things?"

"Yeah, like Johnny Jihad is crawlin' across the sand to get me."

"What sand? Do you see where you are, soldier?"

"I already told ya, I can't see nothin'.."

"How did you know it was me, then?"

"I don' know, maybe your shape, maybe your smell. How long till I get relieved?"

"You'll be on sentry duty through reveille."

The man turned in Brian's direction. "But it feels like I've been in this sand box for years. I'm startin' to think crazy stuff. I'm not ready for this shit."

"I know, Krupkey, I know."

Brian had read the man's nametag off his shirtfront. His head went numb for a minute, mind flashing to his time in Kuwait and Iraq during Desert Storm, to a night out on the rolling plains. As Sergeant of the Guard, he'd checked each post and calmed the boots, Brian as inexperienced as any of them.

They had bivouacked for the night north of the oil fields. He had established a perimeter with Krupkey and Sanders assigned one of the closer-in posts. Sometime after 0100, Sanders reported Krupkey missing. The platoon hunkered down with weapons at the ready and scanned their surroundings with night vision goggles. They saw nothing. In the morning, they discovered boot prints leading from Krupkey's foxhole into the desert where they disappeared. They had never found him.

"Where did you go, man?" Brian blurted. "We spent a full day combing that frickin' desert looking for you."

"I'm not sure...I went anywhere. I can still smell the smoke from the burning oilfields. I've been in this dark place ever since then."

"You can relax, Krupkey. The war's over...well, sort of."

"But I still can't see nothin'."

The soldier raised his M16, his arms trembling, and fired into the forest. The sharp crack of the weapon echoed amongst the trees. "There, I heard 'em again. I know they're out there."

"Who, man, who? The frickin' war is over."

"Not for me."

Brian edged away from Krupkey to the opposite side of the trunk and climbed on, moving quickly so as not to get caught in any crossfire.

5.

He focused on his hands and the branches that passed by, one by one, until the light faded. Overhead, the bottom of some kind of platform blocked out the sun. It encircled the tree trunk, with tendrils of electrical conduit snaking downward into the mist. It reminded Brian of a monstrous jellyfish. Moving underneath it, he found a trap door, yanked it open and climbed through. Some kind of office full of people surrounded him. He stood next to the copy machine, a sheaf of papers in his hands, the machine flashing and clicking away. Overhead fluorescents made everything and everyone look jaundiced.

"Don't just stand there," someone said, "We have a meeting with the client in a few minutes and your presentation better be damn good."

He turned to see Mr. Truesdale glowering at him. "I...I."

"Cut the crap, Brian. This is your project, your design... although I don't think you have clue one about cost or buildability."

"But...but you liked my design."

"Yes, you're quite talented...typical Cornell grad. But, for Christ sake, how can the client possibly afford to build what you've shown me?"

"They're a big company. They have the capital. I want something meaningful, not just another glass box...like this one."

Truesdale scowled. "You know, I designed this building myself."

The back of Brian's neck turned cold and he shivered. "I...I didn't know that."

"Obviously you don't know everything. We came in under budget and ahead of schedule."

"But sir, it's an ugly box. Five years from now, who the hell will care about budgets and schedules?"

"Watch your mouth. Remember who you're talking to. I'm the one that's giving you a chance. So don't crap all over it."

"Yes sir. I just get so tired of architects saying that good design costs too much. That's bullshit and you know it."

"Stop talking, Brian, and finish what you're doing."

Brian looked around him, at gray-carpeted hallways passing

between gray-sided cubicles extending to the horizon. The only sounds came from the click of computer keys and muttered conversations. He slipped into a vacant cubical, picked up the desk phone and tapped in his wife's cell number. His call went directly to voice mail.

"Hey Doris, this is Brian. I'm on some kind of weird...weird trip here...I'll be back with you as soon as I can...."

He took the first hallway on the left and found the men's room. In one of the stalls he stood on the toilet and pushed open a ceiling grate. Sunlight streamed through. He pulled himself upward, his muscles straining, heart thundering, and stood on a massive limb. The roof of the skyscraper stretched out directly below him. The chilled air burned his lungs again. He checked his phone, still no service, and climbed on.

6.

Brian stopped to rub his hands together, chafed from grasping rough limbs and numb from the cold. He patted his jacket and retrieved the silver pocket flask filled with high-grade vodka. He carried it everywhere, would take a nip when things at work or at home got impossible, a frequent occurrence. *Doris is right, I'm a frickin' alky. But so is everybody at one time or another. I still have time for rehab...just not now.*

The booze burned his throat but in a few moments warmed him, relaxed his tight shoulders. He pushed on, eyes barely open, his hands grasping and pulling, one limb after the other. The tree's trunk shrank in size along with the thickness of the branches he climbed onto. Looking downward, the entire pine seemed to plunge back and forth in the wind, ripping holes in the fog. He felt like a sailor, standing in the crow's nest of a tall ship, crossing a wrinkled sea far below, although he couldn't see anything beyond the mist.

Above him, the sky burned the bluest of blues, the sun a

white star. He reached for his sunglasses but couldn't find them. Shielding his eyes, he gazed upward. A small wooden box rested in the crotch of some branches. It swayed back and forth in the wind. Brian thought of the nursery rhyme and quickened his pace. But as he drew nearer, he stopped. Damn, that's not a cradle...it's a coffin.

He climbed onto a limb opposite the miniature casket and rested on his haunches, trying to decide what to do. After emptying the flask of vodka, he reached out and grasped the coffin's lid and pulled. As if gravity and friction had disappeared, the top flew into the air, tumbling end over end, spinning slowly upward, then turning and plummeting downward and disappearing into the fog. Inside the box lay his daughter, Sarah.

Brian grabbed at his chest. The pain of remembrance took his breath away. Sarah had been nine when she died of leukemia after a long battle. He and Doris never tried to have children again, never chancing the return of that particular intensity of pain. And they'd never talked about it, the memories too tragic.

He reached forward and touched Sarah's slender hand. She was dressed in her Sunday best, her blonde wig glistening in the sunlight. Frigid tears tracked his cheeks. Turning on his cellphone, he prayed for bars, for the chance of phoning Doris, to finally share this moment, so poignant in the treetop's thin air. His efforts proved futile.

A strong gust of wind almost knocked him from his perch and he threw his arms around the trunk and sobbed. But the cold wouldn't leave him alone. It seared his lungs. He closed his eyes and climbed on.

7.

The wind died gradually and a cloying silence enveloped him. With half-open eyes he looked upward. There were no more branches, just a spindly treetop. The blue faded in and out, being replaced by the blackness of space and the wonder of the cosmos. Brian glimpsed star clusters and galaxies spinning across the universe, their light so pure that it hurt to look too long. A great force gripped his chest, threatening to crush him like a discarded container. His body felt weightless and he clung to the tree trunk as the heavens sucked at his spirit, pulled him toward the abyss. He thought about the people and situations he had encountered on his long climb. Should I leave them all in the past and just float away? What good is this struggle now?

His cellphone still showed no bars. There will be no shortcuts this time, no phone-it-in responses, no convenient forgettings. He pulled his jacket around his trembling body and forced himself downward. The mist below him receded as he went. He expected to run into obstacles once again, but encountered none. The air warmed and he unbuttoned his jacket and picked up the pace. His lungs filled to their fullest for the first time, giving him energy, confidence, loosening the bands of fear that had gripped him. On the last branch he paused, grabbed the empty pocket flask and dropped it into the mist. After a split second it clinked against something. Brian grinned and stepped off the limb, hitting the ground with a soft thud.

He lay on his back and stared up at ceiling vents. His arms burned from where plastic tubes dripped clear liquid into his veins. Someone wearing a medical mask filled his vision.

"He's back." The woman's voice echoed in the room filled with beeping machines. "How do you feel, Brian?"

"Better," he murmured.

"Good, that's good. The procedure went well. The doctors were able to clear the obstruction. You should recover in a few days."

"My wife…."

"She's right here."

Doris wore a head cap and a mask. She bent over him. Her tears dripped onto his hospital gown. "You scared the hell out of me, honey. Are you okay? Can…can I get you anything? Are you warm enough? You kept saying you were cold, mumbled something about your phone, about climbing."

He closed his eyes. "That can all wait. Just hold me."

He felt her head rest gently on his shoulder as he drifted off. But not before vowing to make contact with all those others he'd encountered on the climb.

CURTAIN CLOSING
NATHANIEL NEIL WHELAN

Go leave me and live your life...

These words ring louder than any gunshot or wail of sorrow. They're blinders, keeping my mind clear. I take deep breaths to control my pulse. Is this really happening? I've spent most of my adolescence wanting to leave this city. Now I can.

A burly figure rams into my shoulder and I topple onto a bench. As I try to orient myself, I watch the passersby looking powerless and shocked as smaller pockets of people squawk angrily at the aggressive display of their government. I push off from the bench and continue onward, passing familiar buildings that mean nothing to me. I have always lived in this city, but it was never my home.

I try to be more aware of my surroundings, dodging frantic looters whose arms are full of stolen foodstuff. I am reminded of the stories my father used to tell about looting during the war. War does certainly seem inevitable. It used to take an invasion or even just an assassination, but now all it takes is a wall.

Popping out of a side street, I begin running parallel along the border. It's a maze of mayhem. Families and friends have been separated now that all exit points have been closed off.

They call to each other, making vows of rescue and confessions of love.

Under the surveillance of their superiors, abused workers with sunken expressions unravel barbed wire while others lay large blocks of concrete as tall as Alsatians. Not one section of border is left unguarded. The entire city has become a prison. I would've heard the commotion if I hadn't stayed overnight at the hospital, but then I wouldn't have been able to say goodbye.

The air is abuzz with the sound of jackhammers tearing up the streets and water canons keeping protestors at bay. Sporadic gunfire makes me flinch, cowering behind useless upraised hands. A young couple charge past heading straight for the barbed wire. One takes a leap like an Olympic jumper and hops her way to freedom while her friend collapses with the echoing staccato of a pistol shot. I duck my head and stare at my feet, avoiding eye contact with the border guards to signify that I am no conspirator.

Before long, I burst through the front doors of my building, scale the stairs to the third floor, and erupt into my apartment. I live in a drab edifice of gray stone, but even still it's more pleasant than most of the tenement buildings deeper in the city.

I curse when I notice Kyland isn't home. To drown out the silence that is usually broken by my roommate's constant blabbering, I fumble with the knob of my radio. Soon the voice of the newscaster blasts past the static and announces that the newly constructed wall is a legitimate defensive manoeuvre on behalf of the Party to protect the city against American imperialist aggressions.

I'm drawn to the window. I live in the east, but three stories down is West Berlin soil. From this vantage point I can see my favourite cafés, shopping plazas, and even the zoo. After the war, all the old commercial districts were revitalized into new sprawling urban developments. It is an oasis of possibility.

A taste of American capitalism in the heart of Germany. But despite being two halves of the same city, East and West Berlin are two different places. Here people scramble for a crumb or a single pinch of salt. There people are more concerned with skin lotions and Hollywood movies.

It is not the voice of the newscaster that pulls me out of my reverie, but the shouts from below my window. A group of West Berliners are calling up, encouraging me to jump. I open my mouth to reply when *Fräulein* Seyferth flings herself out the window one floor below me. With a chorus of *oofs*, they catch her.

Now it's my turn. I tell them to wait, retrieve a cracked leather sack from under my bed, and begin wildly packing what few possessions matter to me. Photographs. Childhood trinkets. My striped rainbow socks. I make a mental note to also collect what's hidden inside the cushion of the beat-up lounger. Thank God, my bandmates in West Berlin already have my Gibson.

My blinders are back up, so I almost don't hear Kyland enter the apartment. His bearlike build casts a shadow over the small living space and his usual kind face is twisted into a frown. It catches me off guard. Are the creases in his forehead from shock? Apprehension?

"What are you doing?" he asks, his voice barely above a whisper.

"Leaving."

"Why?"

"Haven't you been outside?" I ask, then add, *"Dummkopf,"* in hopes of cracking a grin.

"But the border guards…"

I've never seen Kyland so scared. This is a man whose confidence is as unbreakable as the concrete blocks being laid down at the border.

"This might be my only chance to escape. I won't live here like a prisoner."

"This could all blow over."

"I don't care. There's nothing left for us here, Kyland. Go get Klara and let's leave."

Kyland takes a step back and shrinks into himself, gnawing on his bottom lip at the mention of his sister's name.

"But... what about your mother?"

Go leave me and live your life...

I stop packing, shoulders hunched. "I just came from the hospital. We said our goodbyes."

"You're just going to leave her?" His voice is filled with unexpected venom.

The remark hurts. "I stayed in East Berlin to help her through her sickness, but she's only getting worse. She knows it too. Soon she won't even remember my name."

"So, you're not leaving her. You're abandoning her."

"Kyland, why are you making this harder than it already is?" I can feel the sting of tears behind my eyes. "Knowing I put my dreams on hold to care for her is killing my mother just as much as the illness. If I stay, my music career is dead forever and she'll blame herself. She already does. Trust me. This is torture, but it was her idea. She's given me her blessing. Otherwise, I wouldn't be packing."

"But you can play here. I'm sure there's clubs that still-"

"Wake up, Kyland!" I point to the radio where the newscaster is still spewing propaganda. "The police are cracking down harder on rock musicians. There are more arrests than ever. More clubs being raided. The *Stasi* might already have a file on me! It's not safe anymore."

I ignore Kyland's mutterings and lug my sack to the window. It's a long way down, but the group below have fetched a giant bedsheet. Other neighbours are throwing themselves out in a hurry as if spooked by a ghost. Just then I hear heavy footfalls rumble up the stairs. I gaze at Kyland. His meaty hands are clasped as if in prayer.

"Just don't leave yet," he pleads.

"Kyland? What's wrong?"

He makes a desperate grab for my sack. As I fight him off, our apartment door bursts open on rusty hinges. Two *Stasi* agents stand framed in the chipped doorway. They're wearing civilian attire, but their hard stares reveal their identity.

"Dolphus Neumann?" the man on the left inquires in a coarse voice.

I don't hesitate. Abandoning my sack, I sprint for the window, but the burlier of the two agents snags the back of my shirt and heaves me to the ground. One punch to the face and I'm coughing up blood. One kick to the gut and I'm squirming on the floorboards. A nauseating tingle burns in my throat.

Through blurry vision, I watch the second agent flip through my collection of records.

"Mendelssohn... Strauss... Schuman," he recites and turns to Kyland. "Where are the others? The ones you spoke of earlier."

Kyland indicates the cushion of the lounger with a crooked index finger. I recall the time he broke six bones in his hand defending me from schoolyard bullies. That was over twelve years ago. It seems that time has passed.

The second agent retrieves a pocket knife and cuts a scar directly in the middle of the corduroy cushion. His hand dives into the cotton stuffing and pulls out the Elvis records I smuggled across the border. Defeated, I lay my head on the floorboards.

"Yankee-Doodle-Boy," he sneers, eyes narrowed. One by one, he snaps each vinyl in half over a squared knee.

"How could you do this, Kyland?" I ask as the first agent lifts me off the floor and drags me across the room. Betrayal burns on the tip of my tongue.

Through hiccupping sobs, Kyland says, "They have Klara, Dolphus. They have my sister. I'm sorry. They made me tell. They have –"

He receives a backhand slap and is soon out of sight as I'm dragged into the narrow stairwell and down into the lobby.

My head lolls against my chest. A small part of me feels sympathy for Kyland, but he's a fool if he thinks he'll be reunited with his sister if he cooperates. The *Stasi* are ruthless and Kyland just joined their ranks.

A soft ironic chuckle escapes past my split lips. Better to be a spy than tortured by one.

My new life awaits. It's just not the one I expected.

SPACED
JASON D. GRUNN

It still bothers me. I was told that it rarely happens, that the last incident occurred fifty years ago, even then astronauts had fail-safes that worked...

Pack of liars. All my instructors at the Martian Orbital Engineer Academy *lied*. My magnetics didn't hold me to my satellite when I needed them the most after the collision. My tether simply *snapped*.

Why am I still mulling over this?

...

I guess I can't help my reactions, whether I can control them or not doesn't matter anymore, nothing matters anymore.

I was spaced, sent flying into nothingness.

No one is coming for me, no one *can* come for me, or they would have already.

It's already been eleven days according to the green block letters on my transparent HUD.

...

I am going to die.

...

Despite what others might say, grief doesn't happen in stages, in an orderly fashion, humans are just not like that. When I was first jettisoned by the impact of a shuttle going off course, I experienced an acute denial. Then the bargaining, "Someone *has* to come for me, I know it. I just *know* it." Then the anger, "Why is it taking so goddamn long?! Help me!" Next was more pleading, more bargaining, 'Please, please come–I'm sorry I shouted. I just need help, *please...*' It was at that time that I cried more than any other moment in my life, I couldn't say any words as I watched Mars get further and further away from me.

The depression set in after my radio stopped receiving transmissions. I couldn't say anything for a whole few days. All I could do was just slowly turn around once every hour.

Eventually I made a little game for myself, and guessed which way the sun would streak across my helmet. It was hard to guess properly, as the automatic tinting masked the exact positioning of the sun somewhat.

A day later I screamed and cursed and hit my chest and howled and cried and banged my helmet and hyperventilated and screamed and cursed until I passed out from breathing and moving too much.

I woke up a few days later. I felt refreshed, especially after a few long sips from my water tube. My suit HUD showed that I had two liters left, and with the suit recycling my urine I was taught that it could last for at least twenty nine days. The lithium power cell would run out by then. I had to be sparring with the electrolytes, which could filter through the water tube, to keep myself from going insane from hunger. Last time I checked I had about half a liter of the stuff, lime flavored, and my favorite.

...

But now, why even bother keeping track? No matter how good a sleep I get, no matter how good I feel after the rest, the conclusion is still the same.

For the next twenty hours, I sing some jazz tunes to myself as I fiddle with the HUD and its features by pressing on the buttons of my wrist pad. I find a game that I never knew was there before, a classic arcade version of Asteroid. Why the hell not. Now I wish that the academy allowed music for these suits to supplement my digital activity of destroying green polygons on my faceplate. That's odd, if the music was labelled as a "dangerous distraction", then why did they allow a game that takes up your entire view? Then I notice there's no sounds in the game.

To be fair, we needed to listen to orders coming through the radio channels, but flashy arcade game visuals were okay, for some reason.

After beating my high score for the twelfth time, I drift off to sleep again, while drifting in the endless vacuum of space, maybe I could write a poem about that or something...

...

My helmet is beeping.

...

Shut up, I'm trying to sleep.

...

The beeping is still going.

...

Seriously, I'm tired. I don't want to think about dying again just yet.

...

Christ.

My heavy eyelids lurch open to watch the words, "PROXIMITY WARNING" taking up my entire view in red block letters. So…what, is a piece of the satellite I was working on coming out here to finish me off? The possibility scares me a bit, but I prefer to die sooner than later.

An object of some sort partially blocks my view of the sun. I blink several times. It disappears after a few seconds. I think my mind is starting to finally slip. Probably hunger hallucinations. Before going back to sleep, I turn off the damn alarm with a few button pushes on my wrist pad.

...

Something hits me on the shoulder, hard, I yell. My magnetics activate, and the front of my suit sticks to…something.

...

What is this thing?

I have to feel the smooth, dark surface several times to convince me that this metallic surface is in fact, real. I tap it with my fingers, it feels solid. I bang on it with my fist, no vibrations, like I'm hitting a thick piece of pure steel. I kick it. I hit it a few times with my helmet. I shake my head several times, and even bite my tongue and lower lip. I feel blood leak out my mouth. I close my eyes hard, and open them. I repeat it all once more.

...

This thing is real.

Is this a rescue ship? I try all my radio channels, "This is second degree Orbital Engineer

Anthony Ballard, does anyone copy?"

I wait two minutes for a response with each frequency. I try again, and again, and the last channel. I wait.

And nothing. I'm not surprised.

...

Might as well explore it.

I change the magnetics of my suit to operate on my hands, elbows, knees, and feet instead of my stomach. I have to crawl, it's only when I kicked the object that I realized I can barely move. Even with the magnetic assistance and a few big gulps of my electrolytes.

The shape of this thing reminds me of a swimming squid with all its tentacles folded into a thin, oval, torpedo. I can't find any surface features, it's so smooth that I can see my reflection on the side of it.

Humans made this thing, right?

But, why not? I've heard of some scary tech out there. Conspiracy theories aside, I can't find an entrance into this thing. It's not even that big, maybe about the size of your usual passenger shuttle, which can fit about twenty to thirty people. Then something hits me, an idea, not another object.

Did I collide into this thing by chance? Or was it searching for me…

If this was a weapon, I wouldn't even get near the thing. Probably would have vaporized me with a beam of some sort.

My hand sinks into the surface–I retract it immediately. I give my glove a detailed inspection. My HUD doesn't show any suit breaches, my hand doesn't feel any extra warmth or cold, or pain for that matter.

So, I stick my hand in again, got nothing to lose. It just passes right through. Then I get this crazy idea, I stick my whole head into the object.

…

There are lights on in here. I twist my helmet around a full three sixty degrees, twice.

…

I see handle bars among the light blue LED lights. This is a space ship of some sort. Then

I get another crazy idea, I pull my entire self through.

I'm inside, didn't feel a thing. Looking back at the entrance, it appears as a solid wall. I have to look everywhere else.

In front of me is a t-intersection of tubes, one going to the right, and one going to the left.

Both ways are covered in simple black handle bars, white padding of a material I've never seen before, almost like aerogel in a way with its transparent qualities, and several light blue LED lights aligning the floor and ceiling, or ceiling and floor… whatever.

What I find the strangest thing about this…craft I guess, is that there are no symbols or letters of any kind on *any* of the walls I float across. Even with the complete lack of gravity, my limbs feel incredibly limp and heavy when I move them. The crawling around outside must have taken away too much of my stamina. Still, I keep moving through intersection to intersection, looking for anything important, or at least something interesting to occupy my last days alive.

Out of curiosity I check my HUD for any kind of atmosphere.

…

There's breathable air in here. Just the right mix of oxygen, nitrogen, carbon dioxide, and other trace elements, all good for a human to breathe.

…

Then I get yet another crazy idea. I loosen my helmet fasteners, and lift it off. But just in case, I exhaled all my air out to prevent a nasty decompression effect, you never know.

…

I can breathe.

…

I can literally breathe in here. I take in a big, long inhale through my nose. It smells, like a sterile hospital in here. Almost a bit bleachy mixed with some kind of pleasant flowery aroma.

Then I reach out to the nearest handle bar, sit still, and listen.

...

Ok, so there's no sounds in here, just my breathing. I guess whatever systems this ship has are noiseless, does that kind of technology exist these days? Not from my experience. I take a big long sip of my water and tether my helmet to the front of my suit before moving on.

I come across a strange, large circle in the wall. It appears to me as a completely black spot, similar to the entrance way to the ship. So I stick a hand through, slowly of course. Just like outside, it passes through effortlessly.

My next crazy idea compels me to pass through the door–I push myself out immediately at the sight of a large and smooth tube that seemed to jump out of nowhere.

Ok, that was intense. I have to settle down. Will that object come after me?

...

Seriously heart, don't need this right now.

...

That's it, slow down...thank you.

I go ahead and slowly enter the room again. The tube sticks out vertically at me, with one end attached to the wall. My neck twists my head around in circles, looking at the entire layout.

Aside from a few more LED lights, two handle bars, and that same padding material, the only thing different from the rest of this ships interior is the tube. Or...pod?

...

Now that I think about it, I see the faint outline of a person inside.

I float around the room a bit, getting different angles to see this pod from. The strangest thing about it though is how none of the lights in here are reflecting off the pod, but I can still see inside of it somehow, even if only partially.

...

Again, another crazy idea pops into my head.
I touch the pod with my glove.

...

Well that was disappointing. It's been a little while and nothing's happened. Guess it's time to leave the room-

I end up banging my head against one of the padded walls–thankfully it didn't hurt–in surprise as the top of the pod disappears, revealing a...person dressed in a red and yellow and black and white suit.

...

That face isn't human. It's much too pale, and the head shape is almost boxy in appearance. Even though the eyes are shut tight, I can tell they're large. The overall figure of this...thing's body is skinny, skinnier than me, and that's saying something.

It starts scrunching its face as if in pain, then grabbing the air with both hands.

...

Oh my God, it's crying. Those wet streams coming from its

closed eyelids have to be tears.

…

It's alone here isn't it, just like I was for the past eleven days. So I get yet another crazy idea, and hold its hand. It grasps my glove with tender force. I squeeze gently, as if saying with my hand, "I understand your pain. You aren't alone anymore." It cries even more, and starts shaking its head a bit, as if sniffing or inhaling sharply. My eyes feel a bit swollen too right now…

…

Man, I might have no idea what this person or thing is, alien, human, something else, but I never expected to spend my last days alive with another presence. I feel a bit better inside, and start breaking down. I cover my face with my other glove. I don't vent like this very often, it feels strange and embarrassing to me.

…

I'm calm again, refreshed too, like I just woke up from a deep, satisfying nap. My face feels all sticky. The thing/person has calmed down too. It lets go of my hand and crosses it over its chest.

It lifts up its other hand and points a long and pale finger at the door. A small orange light appears in its center. I look back at the person.

"Do you want me to follow that?" I ask and scrunch my eye brows. Why did I ask it in English?

Oddly enough, it opens its shiny black eyes a smidgen, smiles at me, and nods.

"Do you-do you understand me?" I give it a look. It nods again, still keeping that soft smile. Then it jerks its hand repeatedly at the door.

"I guess you need me to follow that light, huh?" I ask. Again, it smiles and nods. Then it puts its pointing hand down, and the top of the pod reappears in an instant, that part made me hit my head against the wall again. My head feels fine though, loving this padding material.

So I float out of the room, and start following this silent, small orange ball of light. It leads me through other tunnels of the ship I haven't been to yet.

...

Man this is taking a while. I thought this ship wasn't all that large. Or maybe I'm just so malnourished and slow to move that it seems like it's taking longer than it should.

Good, it finally stopped. I have to take a few sips of my electrolytes.

So another black door. Might as well...

The orb floats inside, then myself. Another small room, with a semi-circular table or control panel right in the middle made of the same material as the outside of the ship. The orb lands in the middle of it, sinks in, then forms the imprint of a hand in its center, *my* hand. The orange handprint begins to pulse.

...
...
...

I reach out with my glove and go through with another crazy idea.

THE BLUE CARD
NATASHA KIRMSE

She stared at the card in her hand, the soft blue such a stark difference from the creamy white letters she'd received before. Her eyes glanced over the words again, attempting to comprehend the meaning behind them, but her mind remained blank taking in no more than the black against blue. She didn't know how to react. She wasn't expecting this. She was expecting something short but reassuring - something like his last one. It hadn't been long, just enough to get the point across.

19 September, 1942

Dear family,
I'm fine. Sorry for the lack of correspondence. Russia was busier than expected. Headed to France soon. Will write when I can.

With love,
Josef

Those were the letters she liked – well, liked was a strong word. She'd prefer her brother not be fighting at all. It wasn't as though he believed in the cause. From what she'd understood, many of them didn't. But that hadn't stopped the German consignment. That hadn't stopped the war.

Still, they'd adjusted. They continued to get up every morning and go to bed every night. Her father went to work, her mother ran the store out the back window. They did what they could to bring home money, to bring home food. She was only thirteen, so she couldn't quite fill the void of her brother, but she helped out where she could. She took odd jobs, helped her mother with the paint store, tidied around the house. It wasn't money like Josef had brought in, but she'd learned quickly that she couldn't compete with the twenty year old in terms of supporting the family. More could be expected from him. So rather than worry about how else she could help, she ran around the house doing what she could, waiting for the next letter in the mail to see where her brother had now been stationed. The postcards, though constant at first, had become more sporadic. Still, they thanked god for even the shortest letter letting them know he was alright. Unlike her parents, she preferred to live in a world of denial and merely think of it as a trip. While the majority of his class had taken off to the city once they'd graduated, Josef had stuck around to help. When Ana had asked him why he'd simply shrugged and insisted that they took care of him for eighteen years, the least he could do was pitch in for a couple before heading off into the world. So when the letter had come and Josef had marched off in uniform with an emotionless face, Ana decided that this was just his chance to finally see the world. There was no war. There was no fear. It was just one big trip.

She liked to ignore the news for the most part. She knew the important parts – Hitler was an evil soul who was trying to overtake Europe, possibly even the world - not that any paper in Germany would print that. He controlled too much. She didn't agree with his views, but she knew of many in her class who did.

Her parents had taught her and Josef not to discuss politics with strangers. It was one of the first things she'd learned growing up. She'd always liked to think she could avoid the drama of the political world, but unfortunately it showed itself at every turn. And as it became more prevalent, it became harder to hide her fear. It had been easier in the beginning. It started out as something that didn't affect her too much. They'd had to fill out ancestry booklets, but she knew she was German and she had the blonde hair and blue eyes of her father's side of the family so she had nothing to fear. She wasn't overly concerned when her mother with her dark brown hair and green eyes had to write several more pages dating back to family Ana had never even heard of. She'd stubbornly looked the other way when young boys in her class had begun to march around in the uniform of Hitler's Youth. She'd called them fools to their backs, and ignored any advances or friendly gestures. It had been fine. It hadn't affected her. Until Josef was taken. That had been the waking moment in which she'd seen how wrong the world had become. She'd known the brothers of her classmates had been enlisting, but many of them had wanted to fight. Josef was nothing but a peacekeeper. Now he was a soldier.

The day he left had changed things. No longer could she be the youngest child, the spoiled daughter. She was forced to mature ten years in the span of months – weeks. Rushing home from school to work, cleaning and cooking when work was done. Her jobs were endless. She had no time to be a child.

Her mother was always worried. Her father too, but it was her mother you could hear crying into the night. A boy down the street had a father go missing during the Great War; she knew her mother feared the same would happen with Josef. Ana knew her father played the strong one, letting her mother cry. He kept it together and as long as he held back his fear Ana didn't worry. She wouldn't worry so long as her father didn't.

Because Josef was strong. If anyone could win, he could. So she stayed firm in her beliefs and followed her stoic father. He never let a tear fall.

Until now.

The appearance of the blue card had shattered everything they had built in their tireless routine. With a cry from her mother, her father had rushed to her side, his own knees buckling at the words on the page. And after tears upon tears and prayers for safety and health, the two had retired to their bedroom leaving Ana to pick up the abandoned notice and read over the words that had plagued her family.

> **Prisoner Name:** Josef Hans Werner
> **Date of Capture:** 22 November, 1942
> **Location of Capture:** Ardennes, France
> **Camp Name:** Camp Algoma, Idaho, US
> **Condition upon Arrival:** Unharmed

He wasn't hurt. That much could be said. At least not upon his arrival to the camp. Before that who knew what happened? She was aware he'd been injured in Russia just a few months before, so who knew what damage that had left?

She'd always loved to track his travels. She kept count of how many countries he'd trekked across and how long he'd been there for, making notes on a map of his journey. But it was different now. Now he wasn't a soldier. Now he wasn't free. He was a prisoner held in an enemy camp. He was across an ocean in a completely different world. And she finally succumbed to the pure fear and loss that had been prodding at her for the past few years.

He wasn't a Nazi. He wasn't the enemy. But she knew that from this moment on he would be labelled as both. He shouldn't have been there. He should've been in school, studying to become an engineer. He should've moved to Berlin, met the love of his life, settled down with his own family for Ana to visit. He could have done it. But now...

Things wouldn't be the same. Things could never be the same. She knew in her heart that though she might one day get her brother back (and even that she wasn't sure on), if he did come back he wouldn't be the same boy who had played with her in the back garden. He wouldn't be the same boy who had panicked when asking out Sofia from down the street. He'd have seen things, lived through things that no one should ever have to. So she knew this little blue card was the start. It was the beginning of a new man. A new life. And she wasn't sure she'd like the outcome of the story this little blue card had just set in motion.

THE BROKEN CHAIR
LAURA WILSON

Friday, July 24, 2015

It happened.

I was out for dinner with my friend Jenn. I was uncomfortably warm, but I wanted to keep my thick arms hidden under my sweater. The server had just placed our main courses in front of us when I heard a crack. Before I could react, the chair collapsed below me and I landed on the floor with a loud thump. I could feel my face turn red with shame. An uncomfortable silence filled the restaurant. I tried to smile, pretend that I wasn't bothered. It happens, right? Chairs break, no big deal.

But then I couldn't get up. I tried to push myself off the ground, but the broken chair was in the way and my arms were shaking. I tried to reach for the table to pull myself forward, but the table was too far away. I tried to roll myself to one side, but my body was too heavy and I was too weak and I was still stuck in the pieces of the stupid broken chair.

Jenn pushed back her own chair and rushed around the table. She took my hands and tried to pull me up. But Jenn was tiny and I was huge and my body didn't budge. Our server tried to lift me from behind, but even his muscular arms weren't strong enough. Another server came over and between the three of them, they got me standing.

My vision blurred with tears, but I could still see that every head in the restaurant was turned towards me. I wanted to die. I prayed that my heart would give up right in the middle of the restaurant.

"Do you want to move to a booth?" Our server avoided eye contact. He was holding his hands awkwardly in front of him and I realized with revulsion that his hands were probably covered in the sweat that had soaked through my sweater.

I looked at our untouched food. The steaming plate of fettucine alfredo that I had been looking forward to all day. Then I looked over at an empty booth, assessed the space between the bench and the table. I wouldn't fit.

I shook my head. I didn't trust myself to speak. I started to talk towards the door, leaving Jenn to deal with the food and the bill. She didn't try to stop me. I wanted to run out of the restaurant, down the street, far away. But even walking was a struggle. I was breathing hard.

When I got outside, I gulped in the fresh evening air and sobbed. I had parked right outside the restaurant so I wouldn't have far to walk to the door. I got in the driver's seat and rested my head on the steering wheel, afraid some of the other diners would come out while I was waiting for Jenn. The seat was pushed back as far as it would go, but the steering wheel still dug mockingly into my stomach.

It was probably only a few minutes before Jenn joined me in the car, but it felt like forever. She didn't say anything, she just touched my arm gently. I blinked back tears and started the car. When I pulled up outside Jenn's house, she touched my arm again.

"See you later," she said as she got out of the car. There were tears in her eyes.

I loved her for not trying to talk about it, but hated her pity.

My husband, Ben, was sitting on the couch when I got home. He looked up in confusion as I came through the door.

"You're home early," he said. And then when he noticed my face. "What's wrong?"

I dissolved into noisy sobs and sank heavily onto the couch beside him. Thankfully Malia and Chantal, our two daughters, were already in bed.

"I broke my chair at the restaurant," I sobbed, "and then I couldn't get up."

He leaned over to hug me, or at least as much of me as he could. I was so big he couldn't even get his arms half way around my body. I was disgusting.

Ben was overweight too. But he was a normal overweight. The kind of overweight that's acceptable to other people. The kind of overweight that doesn't make people stop and stare and grimace in disgust.

After I had cried myself out, Ben asked if I had eaten before the chair broke. When I shook my head in silence, he went into the kitchen to make me mac and cheese. Two boxes, as usual. He brought it to me on the couch and I ate it quickly, finding comfort in the cheesy warmth.

Ben put Suits on Netflix and by midnight, we had watched four episodes and eaten three bags of chips between us. He kissed me goodnight and I watched him go up the stairs with a heavy heart. During my second pregnancy, he had converted the office into a downstairs bedroom because going up the stairs every day was too much for me. I couldn't remember the last time I had seen my daughters' bedrooms. I couldn't remember the last time I had slept in the same bed as my husband.

I cried to myself in bed and thought about losing weight. But I had tried to lose weight before and it hadn't worked. The last time I went to the doctor, I was 514 pounds. I had no idea how much I weighed now.

Saturday, July 25, 2015

Ben let me sleep in the next morning. He probably felt sorry for me. I could hear Malia and Chantal watching TV in the living room and I pushed myself out of bed. The floor creaked as I walked across the bedroom and I hated the sound. The girls hardly looked up from the TV, so I stood in the doorway for a moment and studied them. They each had a pop-tart in one hand, the box sitting on the couch between them. I imagined how terrible it would have been if they were at the restaurant the night before. And then something even worse occurred to me. What if it happened to them one day? I felt sick. Suddenly, I wanted to rip the pop tarts out of their hands.

I had to admit that my girls were a little chubby. Compared to me, of course, they were tiny. And on them, the chubbiness was just cute. But I had started as a chubby kid and now I was too big to even sit on a restaurant chair. My cheeks burned with shame just thinking about it.

I walked into the kitchen where Ben was sitting at the table, a mug of coffee in one hand and his iPhone in the other. He glanced up when I came in and gave me a sympathetic smile. I leant against the table for a moment to catch my breath.

"I'd like to make some changes," I said to my husband.

He put his phone on the table and looked at me cautiously.

"I want to start exercising and eating better. I don't want the girls to end up like me."

He hesitated. I knew what he was thinking. You've said that before. And nothing changed. But, to his credit, he nodded.

"That sounds like a good idea," he said. "Do you want to plan out dinners for the week?"

And we did. We made a meal plan and a shopping list.

"I can go to the grocery store," Ben said, knowing how much I hated heaving myself up and down the aisles, how exhausted I would be for the rest of the day.

"Why don't we all go?" I suggested, determined that today was the beginning of the new me. I pushed away the tiny voice of doubt that tried to creep in. You've tried before. And failed.

Monday, July 27, 2015

I walked up the flight of stairs to my office on the first floor instead of taking the elevator. When I got to the top, I could hardly breathe. My heart was hammering in my chest and I thought I was going to faint. I held onto the railing and closed my eyes.

"Are you okay?"

My eyes snapped open to see Kevin, one of my colleagues, taking the stairs two at a time. He stopped beside me.

"I'm fine." I flapped my hand at him, hoping he would leave me alone.

"Maybe you should stick to the elevator."

I wanted to punch him.

"I'm fine." I repeated instead and he continued up the stairs, still taking them two at a time.

I felt tears threaten and I blinked hard. I knew my face would still be red from exertion when I got to my office and I didn't want my eyes to be red as well.

Tuesday, August 11, 2015

I gave in. I had been fighting with the girls all weekend, trying to convince them that I would make us dinner for Malia's birthday instead of going out for dinner, like we usually did on one of our birthdays. They complained that we hadn't been out for dinner or had take-out in months. When I realized it had actually only been a couple of weeks, I felt like a terrible mother. I was raising my girls on take-out and burgers.

"I'll make you anything," I said to Malia. "What would you like?"

"I want a burger from The Works."

"How about I make us burgers at home?"

"It's my birthday, mom."

"I know it's your birthday, but we can have burgers at home."

"Chantal got to go out for dinner on her birthday."

"Honey, we're trying to be healthier."

"I shouldn't have to be healthy on my birthday. It's not fair."

Finally, I agreed. We would go to The Works. I wouldn't get a starter and I would get a salad on the side. I didn't have to overeat just because we were going out for dinner.

But then I found myself ordering a whole tower of onion rings as a starter, fries with my burger, and a milkshake for dessert. We had cake at home and while Ben was putting the girls to bed, I ate another three pieces.

When he came downstairs, I was sobbing at the kitchen table. He sat down beside me and took my hand gently.

"It's okay. One bad day doesn't undo all of the good you've done over the past two weeks. Just start again tomorrow.

I nodded and squeezed his hand, grateful for the support, but still aware of that voice in the back of my head telling me that it was pointless. That I had tried and failed before. That I should just give up and be fat for the rest of my life.

Friday, November 2, 2015

After a few months of going for evening walks, I joined the gym down the road. Ben bought the membership for me. I wanted somewhere warm to exercise during the winter and had been talking about it all of October, but kept putting off actually buying the membership.

Walking into the gym for the first time was the scariest thing I've ever done. I sat in the car for a few minutes, wiping my sweaty palms on my pants and trying to calm my anxious breathing. I debated whether to just go home. I could start another day. But how many times had I said that to myself? That I would start tomorrow. It was always tomorrow.

I got out of the car slowly and walked towards the entrance. I caught sight of my reflection in the glass doors and wanted to cry. What was I doing here?

When I walked into the cardio room, everyone stared. I felt my face flush red, but I tried to hold my head up high. Ben and I had looked at different cardio machines online the night before and I had decided that I would try the elliptical. There were ten ellipticals lined up in two neat rows. Four of them were occupied by fit girls with tiny butts. All of them together probably weighed less than I did.

I was about to step onto the elliptical, when I suddenly wondered if there was a weight limit. What if I broke the machine? I looked around in a panic. Should I ask someone if there was a weight limit? Maybe one of the staff. But I didn't want to draw any more attention to myself. Should I just go home?

Instead, I took a deep breath and got on the machine. I started moving my legs. The machine creaked a little and I glanced around to see if anyone was watching me. Most people were now focused on their own workouts but a couple were still looking my way. I pressed the quick start button, turned my music on, and closed my eyes.

It was tough. Compared to the other girls, I was hardly moving. My chest felt tight and I was gasping for air. I managed to do fifteen minutes. I felt like I was going to throw up.

When I got to the changeroom, I caught sight of myself in the mirror. My face was red and my shirt was drenched in sweat. A couple of women stepped out of the shower area wrapped in towels. They looked me up and down and I could see the disgust on their faces. I wanted to hide. I didn't think I would go to the gym again.

"Keep up the good work." I turned to see one of the girls who had been on an elliptical near me. "You'll get stronger and it'll get easier."

"Thank you," I said, feeling tears well in my eyes.

You'll get stronger and it'll get easier became my mantra over the next couple of years.

Monday, July 24, 2017

Two years since I broke the chair. I'm still overweight. But now I'm a normal overweight. The kind of overweight that's acceptable to other people. The kind of overweight that doesn't make people stop and stare and grimace in disgust.

So far I've lost about 300 pounds. I have loose skin on my arms and on my stomach. My body is far from perfect. But I always find something that fits me when I shop. I can chase my daughters up the stairs. I sleep in the same bed as my husband again and I can fit perfectly inside his arms. I can go out to a restaurant without worrying about whether I will fit in a booth or whether the chair is strong enough to support my weight.

I am no longer trapped in my own body. I am providing a good example for my girls.

Breaking that chair was the best thing that ever happened to me.

CURIOSITY
GEORGE TALIN

Adella's bright eyes opened.

"Hey," a voice said. "I can't believe you somehow slept through that."

Adella turned towards Risa, the mission leader.

"Look out there, that's Martian soil."

Adella looked through the window next to her and saw the rust-colored dunes, and the strangest sight: a blue sunset. The hazy orange sky melted into a soft blue horizon. On the ground, several transport vehicles pulled up beside the spacecraft. Adella turned and saw Risa gesturing to hurry up. There was a big problem with the Mars colony, a problem only specialists from Earth could solve.

Adella grabbed her helmet from her locker and attached it onto her suit. Several smaller audible clicks bounced around the corridors of the ship, making her smile—at least she wasn't the last one ready.

By the exit ramp, she found Risa and both of them jumped into one of the transporters, along with a dozen other specialists.

"Hey, Risa," Adella nudged her colleague. "Do you have any clue what the 'big problem' is supposed to be? Why didn't they tell us of any details yet?"

Risa stared into Adella's eyes for a moment, unblinking. "I trust we were sent here for a reason. We'll just have to ask the Colony Director for more details."

Adella sighed. She couldn't wrap her mind around what the Mars-Earth Alliance knew that couldn't be shared with the mission specialists. Each minute, her curiosity grew. Questions kept firing in her mind as they approached Primis, the first and only colony on Mars. There didn't seem to be any issues at first glance. The modular domed buildings looked a bit worn from decades of sand ablating the once-smooth and polished metal. But it was only that, just an aesthetic issue. Not too far from the colony was a large solar panel array, and yet it also looked fine—spotless, in fact. She could see the lights were already on around Primis, so the power was running too. What was it that a hundred specialists from Earth needed to be sent here? Adella became even more puzzled as she realized there wasn't anything in common between them in the team. Risa was an architect, the Alliance coordinator and mission leader. Sitting next to her, Céleste was a botanist specializing in aeroponic plant growth. Adella herself was a specialist in computer systems. Nothing tied them together. Frustrated, Adella wished she could find a clue. She shook her head and sighed again.

They neared the entrance to Primis. All the modular domes of the colony looked as if they seamlessly rose out of the Martian ground. It was as if these massive butterscotch igloos, a marriage of high-tech robotic construction and low-tech earthworks—or marsworks—were curiously formed by nature ages ago. The six domes were connected by tunnels, all to house exactly three and a half thousand permanent Martians. Adella wondered what it must be like to live somewhere so distant from Earth, and not just in a physical sense. What could drive someone to begin a life in a concrete dome on a barren, alien planet?

The vehicle went through the double airlock doors, and Adella could see they were not the first to arrive. A few dozen mission crew members were already inside, and Adella followed her leader out of the vehicle. She looked around the large room they were in, with several floors and platforms connected by metal walkways. Large cargo containers rested against the faraway walls to her left and right.

A man tapped Adella's shoulder.

"Hi, I'm Anthony Markov, Chief of Systems. How was your trip here?"

Adella turned to look at the man. He was neither young nor old, his hair fixed up in a neat ponytail. His bright clothes were a breath of originality after seeing white utility suits for so long.

"Hi, I'm Adella Turing. To tell you the truth, I don't remember much of the flight at all. I must have slept through most of it."

"Adella? That's an interesting name," he said, his eyes were elsewhere. "Where are you from?"

"I'm from England. My parents liked to listen to a popular singer from London, though you might not have heard of her on Mars. When she passed away, I was born, and that's how I got my name. What kind of music do they have here on Mars? I'm curious to know."

Markov lifted an eyebrow, and stared at Adella for a few seconds, without an answer. His face suddenly turned serious. "Are you part of this mission?" He did a lookover of her teammates.

"Yes, of course," she replied. She still wanted to know what music was popular.

"No one else has asked me a question from your team, except you,' he paused for another moment. He looked above at another man on a metal walkway grating, looking over the meeting area.

"I hope we can chat again. Hopefully before your team starts working," he walked away and quickly turned around, "The music here is imported, as are many things... Yet, you might be able to find something here that's uniquely our own." He smiled pleasantly, and his eyes trailed off into a train of thought Adella could sense, but not understand.

She found Risa in the crowd and asked her about the man on top of the walkway.

"That's Walter Hess, Chief of Security at Primis," she said.

Someone approached Hess on the walkway, and whispered something in his ear. The Chief kept looking at the mission team, shaking his head slowly. From the ground floor, Adella thought his expression to be either one of an overworked, tired man or one of cold enmity. She left Risa to take a closer look at Hess' face, just to be sure, when a voice boomed through speakers in the room.

"Hello, this is Colony Director Steve Zhang speaking. Welcome, Earthlings! My, you all look nearly alike with your white space suits. There's no need for them here anymore, the air is pristine, and not a smidgen of radiation. The gravity here, however, is something you'll need to get used to."

Adella spotted the director on top of a platform on the third floor. He had a grey suit on, and glasses that occasionally caught the light, turning them into bright circles.

"The meeting is scheduled to begin in the morning, at 8 o'clock sharp, on the insistence of the Mars-Earth Alliance. You'll be escorted to one of our living quarters shortly. Welcome to our home," Zhang said and exited the room. As he turned off his mic, Adella thought she heard him say something else, the last word being "brief".

When she looked again for Hess, he wasn't there anymore. It seemed odd to her that the Director didn't mention why they were here either. It all seemed too strange, a puzzle which she couldn't solve in her mind. She was determined to find out more about the colony on her own tomorrow morning, before the meeting.

The group of specialists were escorted out of the entrance room, and the living quarters were within reasonable walking distance. Adella tried to speak with the others, but didn't get very far in her conversations. They all would rather sleep instead, and eventually, she decided to do the same.

The time was 6 am, two hours before the meeting. Adella was ready to go explore the colony, when she saw Céleste finish a conversation with Risa. Perhaps she had an opinion on what was going on in the Mars colony.

"Céleste, I'm going for a brief walk to examine the colony for any obvious signs of problems. I could use your help. Could you come with me?" Adella said.

She looked at Adella strangely, and thought for a moment before answering, "I can do that, as long as we come back before the group goes to the meeting. We can't miss it."

"Agreed," Adella nodded. After they were out of earshot from the living quarters, she thought about how to word her suspicions and questions. "Céleste, why did you decide to come to Mars?"

"It was something I was meant to do," she answered without hesitation.

"What is the problem we're supposed to fix here? Everything looks fine," Adella said as she looked around. The colony seemed exactly like something out of a sci-fi movie. Streets were made of smooth hexagonal tiles, the buildings were rounded, and everything was spotless. There was no sky above, as the concrete dome had no windows to the outside world. Quiet electric vehicles drove past them on the wide streets; they didn't seem to be in any rush. People kept their distance when they walked past them. There were no signs of children, but that was to be expected on Primis.

"I'm surprised that you don't know why we're here, Adella."

They both stopped.

"There's an overcrowding issue, and we were sent here to build another adjacent colony."

"Oh," Adella said, looking confused. It seemed so simple, why didn't anyone tell her? She looked around. Was this what overcrowding in a colony looked like?

"We need to head back now, the mission crew is likely getting ready to go to the meeting now," Céleste said.

Adella shook her head. "Wait, I don't understand. How could it be overcrowded if the population here is always maintained? There are always three and a half thousand colonists, and it's been that way for decades."

"The Mars-Earth Alliance is planning to send more of us, and there certainly will be overcrowding if we don't build an extension to the colony in time."

"Why didn't I know about this? This is the first I've heard about this plan," Adella tried to keep herself from shouting, with only moderate success.

"We received an update in the morning, you should have—"

Out of the flow of the crowd, they were suddenly surrounded by a group of men, three in front and three behind them. In their hands, they held metal bars, wrenches, and other tools. One of them simply had a large rock in his hand. They looked at Adella and Céleste with a cold glare.

"Go," another man said behind the men in front. Adella leaned to see who it was, and recognised him instantly: Walter Hess. It was not the face of a tired man, but one of a man consumed by hatred. The men screamed and charged at them. Adella quickly turned and shoved the man behind her, and was surprised by her force. He tumbled, hitting his head hard on the ground, and rolled backwards several more feet. The men near him were shocked for a moment. Adella ran through the opening she made, but as she did, she heard a loud clank behind her, and turned her head. One of the men struck Céleste with a metal bar, and two others grouped around her, hitting her with whatever they had on-hand. All Adella could do was run, and she ran as she never did before. Two of the men tried to run after her, but couldn't keep up. Soon, she couldn't see them chasing behind her anymore.

She found a spot to hide in an unloading area. She hid among the cargo boxes next to a monorail, and tried to figure out what just happened. Why were they attacked? What happened to Céleste? Did they stop, or did they kill her? Why was the Chief of Security there?

Adella's mind chased the questions but came up to dead ends every time. Instead of fear, all she had was a deep sense of confusion. The mission made no sense. The violent attack made no sense—there's never been a violent incident at Mars. She needed to tell the others, quickly.

Adella came out of hiding carefully, but she couldn't tell who could be dangerous. She knew the living quarters weren't far. What if Hess' men were already there? She ran anyway.

When she reached the living quarters, no one was there. No belongings remained, either. The rest of the mission crew must have left for the meeting. Adella headed towards the Elon R. Musk Building at the center of Primis, where the meeting was to take place. Director Zhang's office was also there, and Adella wondered how much she could trust anyone in the colony anymore. Does Zhang know what Hess did?

All seemed normal with the Martians in the colony. The main street was only sparsely being used, and no one seemed to act any different. She received only a few stares, but she expected them, being from another planet.

She arrived at the Musk Building, but still couldn't see anyone from her mission. She went inside, ran up the stairs to the fourth floor, where the meeting room was. The room was empty inside. Did they already finish the meeting? Adella decided to check if Zhang was in his office. She ran across the hall, and opened the door without knocking. He was there, sitting in his office chair behind his desk made of real wood from Earth.

"Oh, hi, your name is?" calmly asked Zhang.

"I'm Adella Turing, one of the specialists sent here from Earth. Where is the mission crew?"

The Director squinted at Adella, and furrowed his brow. His face was painted with a mixture of astonishment and disbelief.

Someone behind Adella called out, "Steve! Hess has lost it. He's about to—"

Anthony Markov walked into the room, and couldn't believe his eyes.

"Look Anthony, how do you explain this?" said Zhang.

"I knew there was something strange going on with her," said Markov.

Adella looked back and forth at the two men. She was tired of not knowing what was going on anymore. She backed up to the windows of the office, and simply asked, "What is going on?"

"You were not at the meeting, Ms. Turing? Oh, my apologies, I take it does not really matter if you are called Ms. or Mr., so excuse my habit. In any case, your colleagues made it short, the meeting only lasted a few minutes."

"What are you talking about?" Adella said.

"You're going to have to tell her everything, Steve. She doesn't seem to be connected with them," said Markov.

Adella threw her hands in the air in bewilderment.

"Yes, I suspected it. Ms. Turing, do you not find it strange how you happen to know where to go on Mars? How did you find my office without your group, on a planet you have never visited before?"

Adella was silent.

"Furthermore, another one of the crew members was absent at the meeting. I do not know who, but I know that only ninety-eight out of a hundred were present. Would you know anything about that, Ms. Turing?"

"Yes, that would be Céleste. Your Chief of Security ordered an attack on us. I don't think Céleste survived," Adella said.

Zhang looked at Markov, who shrugged and shook his head slowly. Zhang nodded.

"I am going to ask you a quick question, Ms. Turing, please answer it swiftly as well. This is for my curiosity. You are walking down a beach and—"

"Does the colony have beaches? I was not aware of it," said Adella.

"No, not on Mars. You are back on Earth, and walking down a beach, when you see a child flapping his arms wildly in the water. He is clearly drowning—"

"Why would he go into the water if he can't swim?" she asked.

Zhang sighed. "Well, that's what's happening, and he will die soon. You are standing there, looking, but not helping. Why is that, Ms. Turing?"

"Because I shouldn't go in the water."

"Why not?"

"It would harm me."

"But humans can go in the water without harm, can they not?"

"Clearly, only if they know how to swim. What are you trying to say?"

Zhang shook his head. "You are not human, Ms. Turing. Neither is anyone from your team."

Adella looked at Markov, who raised his eyebrows, smiled and nodded.

"What? Then what am I?" Adella looked down at her hands.

All seemed normal.

"It is quite interesting how you keep asking questions; it is as if you are as curious as a human. It is fascinating, since you are an android. Your team was simply acting on the programmed orders of the Mars-Earth Alliance. They did not come here to help us with anything, much to my disappointment," said Zhang.

"Do you even know why you are here in the first place, Adella?" said Markov.

She glanced at both men. "No."

"This is what we learned from the Alliance at the meeting. You're part of an initiative to begin replacing all of us humans on Mars with androids who will never rebel. See, you might not have this in your flash drive, but we here on Mars are planning to declare our independence from Earth soon, on New Year's Eve, 2100," Markov paced around the room as he spoke. "It will be a new beginning for us, only thirty sols away from today. Well, the Alliance wants to establish zones of control on Mars instead. All the powerful members are in agreement, which means if they have their way, we'll have separate zones of control for China, the U.S, the EU, Russia, Japan, and India."

"It will be a disaster," said Zhang. "They stopped human flights once they found out there was an illegal birth on Mars. That was when tensions rose. Of course, I have a nagging suspicion all the precious ore deposits that were discovered near Olympus Mons might have also played a role. They want to start mining near the largest volcano in the Solar System, all so some businessman on Earth could claim to be the first trillionaire."

Markov approached Adella, studying her visually. "You look very similar to all the others in your crew. Yet, you're the only one who asks questions. Why is that?"

"I don't know," Adella shrugged. "Why can't anyone else ask

questions?"

Zhang jumped out of his chair and looked out the window of his office. "There he is, the mad man."

Adella and Markov turned to look. An excavator barreled down towards the mission crew's living quarters without slowing down. It crashed into one of its walls, sending chunks of pressed Martian soil tumbling all over the street. It continued by backing up, and ramming the building, over and over, until the whole structure collapsed and turned into broken rubble.

Far away, on one of the connecting streets, were all of the remaining mission members. They appeared to be running, the view partially obscured by a few buildings. Upon closer inspection, they weren't running away. The group was running towards the excavator, which already had a large crowd of local supporters around it. The whole crew broke into a sprint, their legs were a blur, and they charged at the crowd with inhuman speed. The native Martians outnumbered them, but it was immediately clear the clash was one-sided. With unbelievable force, the androids handled the Martians like ragdolls, throwing them around, separating them and tying their hands with a cable or wire.

"There are less than a hundred of them, and they are already taking control of the colony. What will happen when thousands more are to come in the next few years? What will become of us?" Zhang closed his eyes, and rubbed his face tiredly. He suddenly looked like a man who lost everything, whose world was turned upside down in an instant.

"But Adella is here. Why isn't she down there with them? Something doesn't add up," said Markov.

"I don't know what to say. I don't understand how I could be different, but I'm dying to know," she said.

Markov gently turned Adella's head around to check the back of it.

"What are you doing?" Adella snapped.

"One moment," said Markov. "You have four connection slots in here, and one of them is a Mars Universal Port. Steve, do you have a spare MUP cable hooked up to your computer?"

"Frankly, I do not know—check for yourself. What are you trying to do?" Zhang asked.

Markov led Adella to Zhang's computer. He found the cable he was looking for immediately.

"Adella, I'm going to check if there's anything anomalous with your software. You'll have to allow me access, as you're the administrator of your system. Will you do that for me?"

Zhang sighed. "They have pretty much dealt with the crowd. They've grouped them and tied their hands. Brutally quick and effective, your colleagues are," he kept staring out the window, paying no attention to what the other two were doing.

Adella answered Markov without much thinking, "Yes, I am curious to know. Go ahead."

Markov connected Adella to Zhang's computer, and as soon as access was granted, his eyes scanned the screen, starting with Adella's software update history.

"Hah! Would you look at that," he kept studying the data.

"What?" Adella almost turned around, but then felt a tug at the back of her head where the cable was connected, almost disconnecting from the computer and corrupting her data.

"There's a failed software update. It was supposed to disable Module40, and here, the operator's notes were that it 'conflicted with M.E.A commands'. Module40 is... Let me check your hardware manager. Hold on, Adella, your operating system isn't intuitive to me. Are you sure you're not actually a human female?"

Zhang chuckled. "Anthony, you are a scoundrel for making me laugh at a time like this. What on Mars are you doing?"

"Got it. Module40 is responsible for curiosity levels, and decision trees in uncertain situations," said Markov.

Zhang turned around and looked at the window. His expression turned severe. "They are coming here. All of them."

Adella shook her head. "So that's all that separates me from them? Curiosity?"

"No," Markov rubbed his chin. "Seems like they noticed the module interacts with your personality in unexpected ways. I also found out they tried to disable it during your flight here, and I have the frequency channel they used. I'm willing to bet it's the same one for all of your colleagues, too."

"That is all fine and interesting, you learning about these androids, Anthony. However, there is not much time left for us. The MEA has won," Zhang turned around and slumped down against the glass windows.

Adella felt the back of her head, letting her fingers run along the other three connection ports. "Without these, I would be human?"

Zhang smiled, and shook his head.

"I can send the signal that was supposed to turn off Module40 for you over our radio transmitter, but instead modify it by turning off all the modules. Every android will shut down. But, this also means you will shut down, Adella. And once you do, I won't have access to your system anymore, as you won't be able to give me admin access. I'm afraid I would not be able to turn you back on."

Silence consumed the room. It was a hollow, frightened silence, begging anyone to speak only a single word to break it. But the silence stayed, until it was gradually lifted by a sound coming from below, a flurry of footsteps hurrying somewhere.

"They are here," muttered Zhang.

"It's up to you now, Adella," said Markov. "I have everything ready, except your permission to export the command from your system. What will it be: turn everyone off forever, including yourself, and keep our colony independent by doing so, or, stay alive, and let Earth decide what's best for Mars?"

Adella tried to resolve the conflict in her mind. She ran the hypothetical paths into thousands of different directions, but she couldn't figure out which decision would produce the most positive outcome. Her thought process kept branching into different possibilities, cycling them into an infinite spiral of hypothetical decisions and futures. She was overtaken by the desire to know more, and to figure out which decision would add up to being the right one.

The footsteps clattered along the stairwell, getting louder with every second. The harrowing sound was like a mix of soldiers marching, and metal bumping against metal.

Adella could not resolve the unending decision trees. But, she was curious to know what would happen with a decision no other android could make.

"Yes, Markov, go head," she declared.

Markov hit a button on the keyboard, and covered his mouth in his hand. His eyes stared at the screen, unblinking. "I don't know if this will work or not," he said.

Adella turned to look at Markov as much as she could. "I hope it does," she said, "I really want to know what happens to Mars when—" her head dropped to her chest, and she toppled to one side, falling with a heavy thud on the floor.

Several androids sprinted into the room, and then froze midrun, crashing into Zhang's desk with incredible force. Markov barely jumped out of the way, as the weight of several androids smashing into the desk broke it apart. The first few had enough momentum to smash into the wall behind the desk, filling the air with rock dust. The sound of inactive androids falling down the stairs echoed through the room.

The dust settled, and Zhang and Markov rose to their feet, shaken but unharmed apart from scratches and bruises. They looked around the room. It was a mess full of broken furniture, android bodies, and dust covering the floor. In the middle of it all was Adella's body, turned to one side with a ripped cable hang from the back of her head. Markov turned her over, and saw the last facial expression frozen on her face, the beginning of a gentle smile.

THE MOTHER'S END
JENNIFER NG

I imagine your loneliness as you stared at the water. Your fingers have wrinkled, and your laugh lines have deepened. The world doesn't notice you. The Pacific Ocean stretches far beyond what the eye can see, and you stood lost in its vastness at the beach, digging your toes into the sand. This ocean understands me, you think. A cool wind brushes your arms, and you shiver. You and I know the deep sorrow caught in your bones.

You don't want your friends and family to think that you didn't try. You left Taiwan where you lived off your family's wealth. You returned to the city of San Francisco to survive on your own. This is the city where you spent your youth, dancing at tiki bars and crashing dinner parties. You walked the streets up and down like you did in your twenties. You smiled. You volunteered at the Ronald McDonald house. You found your old friends—complimenting on their fashion taste and inviting them to extravagant dinners. But your friends have moved on in their lives. Their bones ached, and their bodies preferred quiet nights. Looks from strangers' eyes burdened you as you navigated the world without the assured beauty of your twenties. You noticed your bank account crashing toward emptiness. You applied to drive for Lyft, Uber, and Chariot. You loved talking to your passengers. Yet, you knew something was missing, and a weight grew in your chest. You fell into an abyss, strapped with a darkness that you could not fight.

You had a long life— the drama of youth, the tumult of motherhood, and a never-ending yearning for wholeness. Years of history tumbled out like weeds in your hands.

The sun dims, and memories rush through your head. You remember the fight with your daughter, when you hiked alone without telling anybody. A light drew you to the crest of a hill while your daughter fiddled with the car. You walked toward the light, hoping that it would fill the hole inside you. Thorny bushes and rough gravel didn't stop you, and you reached the crest after an hour. The sun shimmered among the clouds. Its light beamed upon trees, red-roofed houses, and bucolic hills. When you returned to the car, your daughter pounced on you, demanding to know where you went. In between her long breaths, you told her about your walk and the light. It's so beautiful, you said, it's so wonderful. How could she not understand the beauty that filled your heart?

You must always protect your children. When the oldest was four, you called the fights with your ex-husband: "little disagreements". Everyone has them, you told your oldest. You can't agree all the time. How dare he tell you that you lack responsibility? How dare he withhold the letters containing money from your family in Taiwan? How dare he take advantage of your situation? You left him and took the children. Divorce was a godsend. He was furious because he wanted the relationship to work. He tried, but so had you. You wanted to jump out of the cage that he created. Twenty years later, he attended your middle daughter's wedding with his new wife. Anger consumed you when you realized that he found happiness. Bitterness twisted around your remaining energy like a snake, filling your mind with poison. You never married again. You lived a life, moving across the United States, driven by your own desires. At the end of the ceremony, you demanded that your daughter takes you home. But your middle daughter protested, I can't. You ask your other children to take you home. We're hundreds of miles away in Vegas, they said. Let's go dancing, you said, craving a beat of your former youth. We're tired, they said, leaving you to return to their rooms. So you wandered the concrete sidewalks, following a path lit by the neon signs that stretch for miles. You loved being among the crowds, but it was so lonely being alone.

I have seen you a handful of times, and your fire burned brightly every time. I am only a bystander, a recent visitor to your grand life. Yet I sensed your fear stemming from disappointment, failure, and rejection. Freedom is not the same now.

So you stand on the water's shore. The water laps at your feet, beckoning you. It's warmer than you expected. So you walk further in, and the water surrounds you, like a long hug, clinging to your clothes, your shoes, and your hair. Your children are strong. They will survive. Their father will take care of them. For now, it's you. All you, seeking freedom for a new beginning.

THE DARKEST PART OF ME
BRICE PETERS

Dreams, dreams are interesting. Some people believe they are our connection to the spirit world, where we can see dead relatives, connect with god. Some believe we can even see parts of ourselves that are otherwise hidden within.

When I woke up, none of that was relevant. The sickness coursing through my body felt as if my very blood was made of molten lava. The only thing keeping me from bursting into flames was the very sweat my body produced to douse the fire. I would go to whatever spiritual realm or state of consciousness it would take to escape this ailment.

My eyes opened slowly, with great effort. The first sight that met my eyes was an unkempt room, messy and disorganized. The carpet was folded over, papers coated the desk in the corner, and clothes covered every surface. The room was poorly lit. I was unable to see what the rest of the apartment looked like, but I knew it wasn't mine. It was hard to remember anything else, my name, who I am, where I am, and how the hell I got here. The only thing I knew was the date. August 30th 1888. The first thing I had to do, was get up.

I stood up out of bed. It felt like clubs had bludgeoned every bone in my body. The cracks they made were wet and dull, each one reminding me I was only a man, at the mercy of my body. After one step forward, and much stumbling, I made it to the curtains and drew them back, revealing the pure powerful white light that was so strong it could have purged even Satan's darkness in hell. I was forced to close my eyes to the light and blinked furiously to adjust. After my encounter with God, I was able to see the beautiful city of London. The pale grey streets, the people bustling like ants, and good old Big Ben. The tower was so tall, you'd swear it could reach heaven itself. It was also great to see the time. It was already noon. The need to get dressed was already taken care of, I must have fell asleep in my suit. I looked away from the city, trying to fight off the fog concealing my identity.

I closed my eyes trying to remember anything, anything at all. I didn't even know where to begin. I felt utterly hopeless and lost, trying to piece together memories when there were no pieces to put together. The sick feeling didn't help. All I wanted to know at this moment was where I was.

I began to look at the room more closely. The walls were a chipped blood red, the part of the floor that didn't have any sort of rug on it was old wood, painted gray, and coated with dust. The rug looked white but had a mixture of stains, making it a horrible shade of brown. It was almost repulsive. The clothes that covered the rest of the floor produced more questions than it did answers. My eyes were drawn to a scandalously small blue dress. "This can't be mine," I mumbled. "Much too small, and definitely not my colour." The dress laid on the floor carelessly, as if it had been thrown onto the ground.

I picked up the dress, a very tiny thing. I imagined it was meant for a more provocative, sinister purpose than just mere clothing. A flash of anger quickly flooded over me like a wave, pulling me beneath the waters of thought and into the dark depths of fury. The anger was so quick and intense it scared me. I shook my head and said almost apologetically, "It's just a dress." I tossed it back on the ground as I had found it.

I looked over to the desk, searching for more information. Walking became easier as the fog of sleep slowly drifted away. The desk was old, possibly an antique. It was possibly the only nice thing in this apartment. Made of a dark wood, without any sign of damage to it. It appeared to be covered in letters. I picked up a few of them. After quickly skimming them, I saw that all of these letters were addressed to the mother of the woman, whose name, I learned, was Faye. In the letters, Faye mostly described her financial issues and rent troubles, and inquired about her mother's well being. There was no hint of me, no man's name mentioned whatsoever. We must not have known each other for long. My gaze was drawn, as if by a siren's song, to a picture. The picture was of Faye, or at least who I presumed was Faye. She was beautiful, dark hair, and her smile gave a warmth in my heart, like a blanket on a cold day. She looked healthy, and well looked after, with her complexion bright and clear eyes. I caught myself smiling, and reached out to pick up the photo to investigate it more closely. I cradled the photo gently in my hands, and brought it closer. "Where are you Faye?" I started, softly. "I would..." But before I could finish, my body seized, my vision went blurry, then black. I succumbed to the darkness once more.

I collapsed onto the ground suddenly, uncontrollably. As my head hit the floor, the convulsions began. It was as if the devil himself was ripping my soul out, kicking and screaming, taking me down to the dark depths below, where only God could know what lay within. I could feel my mouth begin to foam and saliva poured down my face. When would it end? I thrashed as if to try to stop. After what seemed like an hour, my muscles relaxed and my head stopped hurting. My eyes were still closed, recovering from the pain. Then, all of a sudden, clarity. It came in the form of images, memories. I was with Faye last night. I met her on the street. She seemed nice, friendly. Just what I wanted, what I needed. What I craved. A friend. Maybe more? The way she smiled breathed a new life into a previously lifeless existence, erasing all my worries.

I asked Faye if I could escort her to dinner. Faye, with her smile said, "You're not from around here, are you? You don't have an English accent."

I smirked. "No. I came here three years ago to complete my schooling to be a doctor." Faye looked impressed, and even more interested in learning about me. "Well, sir, I would love to join you for dinner. Mr....", I quickly introduced myself. "Fallow, John Fallow. But please just call me John". The memory ended abruptly.

I opened my eyes and reality quickly set back in. With the last of the emotion from the memory fading into the black of my mind. "At least I know my own name," I said begrudgingly. There was nothing else to explore in the room. It was time to leave, see what else I could find. Starting with where I took Faye to dinner, if only I could remember where that was.

I stood up, and as before, it was just as painful and exhausting. I was up on my own two feet again at the least. I wiped the spit from my face onto my sleeve. I began to adjust my shirt, and winced. I gingerly pulled my shirt up, and realized that the pain may have had to do with the severe bruising, extending from my lower ribs to the top of my hip. It was colored like a ripe, purple grape. "Oh, bollocks!" I exclaimed with disbelief. After staring at the injury for a few more seconds I tucked in my shirt, feeling the electric pulsing pain course through my body with each adjustment I made. I walked to the door and opened it. After one last glance at the apartment to see if there was anything I had missed, I walked out the door, letting it fall shut behind me.

By the time I had exited the building, the sick feeling was non-existent. There were people crowding the streets, each trying to complete their own daily tasks. There were orphans on the corners, some begging, all hoping to get a copper so they could feed themselves for another day. Others could be seen waiting for one of the many horse drawn carriages to drop something, anything, just to try and use it or sell it. Anything to survive. The other orphans, the ones that weren't in plain sight, the ones that blended into the crowds, they were the real nuisance. The pickpockets. Those brats would steal the clothes off your back without you even noticing, and without a scrap of remorse, too.

Anger boiled inside my veins again, but this was explainable, rational. These cretins could take anything of value, be it of actual or sentimental. Leaving a struggling bloke more desperate, making them more likely to do it to another. No wrong will be without consequence, be it another wrong or justification I thought to myself. Others on the streets seemed to all be like one another, ladies and men. There were some men that were in business attire, nice clean and pressed suits, top hats, most had pantaloons while others demonstrating clearly more wealth had breeches. Others clearly dressed for factory work. Having only trousers, their boots and cap on their heads. The workers made it obvious if they had children, they were almost always by their father's side on the way to work, even for the same job.

While I was watching people rush through the streets a particular event caught my eye. A boy, clearly having disobeyed his father, was being beaten in the streets. The boy cried, "Father! I didn't" he was cut short by another pelt across his face. His father shouted "Stealing bastard! We needed that to eat!" he continued to beat the poor boy until his eye beginning to swell. I thought to intervene, to stop this father from further causing harm. But it was not my place. I put my head down and continued on my way to find where I might have taken Faye. I looked down the street, and just began walking.

There was no true direction or method to my madness. Only my wits and intuition. As I walked I continued to think of the boy being beaten. As I recollected this event, the father looking like he carried the wrath of god behind his fists as he beat his child, that I began to feel a sense of dread. My muscles began to feel odd; I feared another episode might occur. I did not want to draw unnecessary attention to myself if it occurred.

I rushed into an empty alley, just in time as well. I slouched down and let the ungodly event occur. My muscles seized. The pain returned to me, just as strong as ever. My mouth began to foam again. I felt my eyes roll back into the back of my head, into the abyss of my mind. I cannot recall what happened when I entered the darkness, but all I know was it was quiet, silent as if I had died and been laid into the crypt, and awaited my judgment. Soon this darkness filled with my memories, not of Faye. They were of myself, back in America where I grew up.

***

My family and I lived in a small house just an hour's journey outside Louisville. The house was on a small plot of land with a few animals. My father worked hard as a laborer, digging ditches. My mother raised us, and cared for the house. I was so young and naive, then. One day, when I was eight and not helping my father dig, I was out walking around the lush forest that surrounded us. I loved exploring the beautiful woods, investigating for anything interesting. I remembered looking upon the earth, and seeing a dead bird. It was so little and frail, still beautiful in death. Its feathers were clean, I imagined its songs, its music, bringing joy into the silent forest. But what made me curious was, what was on the inside? What gave life to the creature? This question filled my mind, it was all I wanted to know. I carefully picked up the bird, and brought it to the clearing, no closer than fifty feet to the house, but under the cover of the brush. There was a stump concealed behind the thicket where a tall oak tree once stood. We had cut it down for firewood. I carefully placed my obsession onto the smooth stump and rushed to the house.

I crept inside, careful to not draw any attention to what I was doing. As I opened the door the roaring argument raged into my ears. Mother and father were arguing again in their bedroom with the door closed. "You told me we had no money for food, yet I find money hidden away behind the baseboard of the bed! How did you get this, woman?!" His words were loud like a gunshot, and were full of pain, like he had taken a bullet to his heart. "I don't know how it got there! Honest!" my mother cried, her voice filled with fear. "Lies! I know what you've done! To me! To poor John, for Christ's sakes!" his voice broke slightly; I had never heard my father get this upset, this emotional. He had always said to 'leave the emotion for the women'. "The other women, they lie! Don't believe them!" mother cried. There was a silence, brief, but seemed to last eternally. My father replied in a voice that was not his, but that of a broken man, "I didn't believe them, that's why I had to see for myself to be sure. I went to town yesterday afternoon by the tavern, and I saw you by the Millers brothel. You whore!". Father fell silent, and his mother wept. I was devastated; my mother worked in the brothel. It was a disgusting, filthy place where the people who went there were no better. My blood boiled. She betrayed my father, myself. God. My mother, the whore. The sinner. She was surely destined for hell.

"I hate you, " I mumbled, to her. It was all I could muster at this point. I decided to get what I came for; I went to the kitchen and took a small knife from the counter, and left the house again to return to my fascination.

I didn't know what to expect when I opened the dead bird, a ghostly soul lying within, and a bright light? Instead I found the insides to be squishy, any blood that had been there was dried up and to make it worse, the maggots had gotten into the bird. It reminded me of my parents marriage. Something that once seemed so pure and beautiful rotted, leaving an empty vessel full of maggots. The one thing I remember the most about the whole experience, was that I felt nothing, no remorse or guilt about cutting the bird, or killing it the day before. I was amazed that this was all that it took to make this creature function. I expected so much more.

I returned to the house later that day. I saw my mother sitting in the kitchen, she looked at me, and I dared to not look back, and went to see my father. He was in the living room, staring at the floor in distraught. I waited for a few minutes; I didn't know what to say. What could be said when you have your heart stabbed by the person whom you care about most? What could be said that would undo the damage that had been done?

" I love you papa," I said quietly. He said nothing. I turned to leave when he said, "Your mother is sick. She's a very sick woman, John." I paused, and retreated to my room. All I could think about as I laid in my cot, was my father telling me that mother was sick, his voice vibrated in my head like a ghostly whisper that wouldn't stop. I hated my mother at that moment, but maybe, just maybe, she could be cured. If she was cured that could fix everything, and sew shut the open wounds of this family.

The sun set and darkness swallowed our world. It was silent everywhere, nothing could be heard anywhere. Even the air seemed still. I remained awake, laying on my back. I became frightened as the silence lasted, the only thing that broke the intense silence even remotely, was my ears thudding louder and louder as my heart beat harder. I knew, I knew something was coming for us all. I didn't know what, but it was something terrible. Like glass, the silence was shattered and I heard my mother scream, I rushed out of bed to the kitchen. There was my mother, cut her open for the world to see. She was dead in seconds. My father had stabbed her. There was no madness in my his eyes, just pain and anger. His words echoed in my head again "your mother is sick, she's a very sick woman". The echo was deafening, it was all I could hear. It dawned on me, he was trying to cure her. She was sick, that was all.

***

I awoke to a man shouting, "Give 'im some air! He needs air!". So much for not wanting to draw attention I thought begrudgingly. Thank God he sat me up, I did not want to have to fight my muscles to stand up again. "Good sir, we thought you be possessed by a spirit. Let me get you to the doctor. Mr....?". The mans overwhelming kindness to a stranger brought a smile to my face, "Fallow, and no thank you sir, I feel quite alright. It is just a recurring event unfortunately. I will live.". The man opened his mouth to protest, but appeared to change his mind. "Alright Mr. Fallow, godspeed." The man said, and disappeared into the streets without another word. I continued my walk, passing through the alley and into the street.

I walked for hours, attempting to find a clue to where I met Faye, where I took her to dinner, or even where I last saw her. My stomach rumbled and gurgled out of hunger. I needed some food and drink; looking at Big Ben I saw that the time was three o'clock in the afternoon. I began to wonder if I even had money, which brought the realization, I had never checked my pockets for any clues. It was almost comedic at how many clues I may have had, but had never even bothered to look. After rummaging in my pockets I found a pocket watch, some copper, and a necklace. This necklace was not mine, it had to be Faye's. It was a bright green jade stone, cut into a rectangle that had the perimeter neatly covered by copper.

This didn't give me any further clues however, and thankfully no more goddamned seizures. I pocketed the necklace and walked toward the tavern that lay directly ahead. My legs had grown tired and weak from all of the walking. The cobblestone was a bloody pain, I couldn't imagine how the horses that walked on it managed.

I walked into the tavern, it was not busy. The barkeep and his son were working behind the bar, and a young lady was serving drinks to the only other two people who were around. I sat at a table. The young lady looked over, and came over promptly. "Good day to you sir. Can I get you a drink? Or some bread to eat?" she said with a smile, "Good day madam, and yes please I will have both, water please." She nodded her head and smiled, disappearing behind the bar.

While I waited, I pulled the necklace out of my pocket again, looking for anything else to let my memories come back about Faye. I began to imagine her waiting for me with that smile, the intoxicating smile and her eyes that I would get lost in like the labyrinth of the Minotaur. "Excuse me sir? Mr. Fallow? Is that you?" a deep unknown voice asked. I turned sharply, to see who knew me, it was the bartender. A tall muscular fellow with a large grey handlebar moustache with grey messy hair to match. His apron had many stains on it, his clothes appeared to fare no better. "Yes sir, beg your pardon, but who are you?" I replied quietly, I was very intimidated by the sheer size and musculature of this man. What if I owed him money? What if I wronged him? I knew if I had done either of these things, I would be seeing god soon.

The man's reply sounded as if it were thunder "It's Winslow, I recognize you from the past night, you were here with your beautiful lady. I understand you not remembering me, you only had a pint between the two of you, but it's me job to know my customers. Gotta keep 'em coming back." This man seemed quite honest, maybe he would know about Faye? I quickly asked "Winslow, I am looking for that woman you saw me with last night, to return her necklace she had misplaced with me. Do you know where we went to after we had left here? Or where I may find her now?" Winslow stared at me for a moment, hopefully attempting to remember something useful. By the looks of him though, it didn't look as if he could remember what he had for breakfast this morning. Winslow than just slowly shook his head and said "Sorry sir, all I remember was you two paying your tab and leaving. My reason for approaching you was to give you this". Winslow outstretched his arm and revealed in his hand a small bag. I didn't know the contents of what was in the bag, I prayed it was something useful, but what the hell could be in this "You dropped this on your way out, I didn't look in it" Winslow said, almost as if he expected me to call him a thief or a snoop. "Thank you Winslow," I said quietly.

I took the bag in my hand, it had some weight to it but wasn't too much of a burden. The barmaid returned with some bread and a glass of water. "Excuse me gentlemen" the bar maid said as she placed the food on the table and the glass of water beside it. She turned suddenly and snapped "Winslow, how many times have I asked you not to pester the guests? They won't come back if you keep smothering them! Go back behind the bar with your son!" her scorn was fierce, and was almost comedic with the effect it had on Winslow. I expected the woman to be shunned away, and maybe even hit. Winslow is a giant that could wrestle a horse to the ground with ease. Yet this tiny woman cut him down with a matter of words. "Yes, love," Winslow replied and walked back to behind the bar. The barmaid followed. As he walked by I thanked him and began to eat slowly.

While I was eating I tried to think of where I might have gone with her. Very little possibilities came to mind, I couldn't focus, my memory was in ruins. I took a drink of water, and a bite of my bread. Nourishment was just a chore, an aggravating task. I felt a twitch in my muscles, and a brief pain shot through my brain. "I swear…" I muttered, I did not want another seizure, and to my surprise, it didn't occur. I began to remember, and did not end up flailing on the ground like a harped fish.

My mind wandered to after the death of my mother. My father and I labored daily to make as much money as we could, and it was a way besides church that I could spend time with my poor father. He never truly recovered from my mother. Through hard work and a series of miracles I trained under the local doctor, who saw I had a talent for medicine. He had a colleague in London where I was shipped.

***

There was so much to learn. People were simple creatures but there was so much to know about how we worked and what was the machinery in our body that allowed us to function. I remembered my very first patient that I had encountered in London. This woman rushed into the local doctors house, the one I had been apprenticing under. He had stepped out to visit a patient who had been kicked by a horse.

The woman entered the house begging for help before seeing no one there but myself. She asked if I was a doctor, when I confirmed she hurried me to a house across the road. She quickly rushed me to the basement. "My sister please help my sister!" she screamed. A woman, I assumed was her sister, lay flat on the floor. I crouched down to examine her, she appeared to be in good condition. Her body was unmarked, no sign of injury. I had no idea where to even begin to help this woman. "How did this happen?" I asked authoritatively. "She just collapsed, she had said she felt under the weather" the woman cried. "What kind of activities has she been doing?" I pressed. The woman fell silent, her hysteria turned to shame in a matter of moments. "Speak dammit! I can't help if I don't know what I am up against!" I yelled, this woman was testing my patience. Tears poured down the woman's face and she began to sob, "She…." The woman took one more look at her sister as if whatever she was about to tell me was worth as much as her sister's life. She finally said "she has been low on money, so she has been working in a brothel," the woman sobbed uncontrollably at that moment. My motivation to help this woman faded, and was replaced with a much more sinister emotion, anger. Prostitutes, they break hearts and prey on the desires of men, extorting our weakness of the flesh. I remembered my poor father, after my mother broke his heart, the empty shell he became, the justice he brought down on her, and finally ending his own life after I came here to London. I looked at the woman, "I will be right back". I left the house and went to the doctor I was apprenticing under and informed him of the situation. He saved her life, but not her soul, there's no true saving prostitutes except through God's saving grace. I would have no part in saving the wicked or the damned.

***

I finished the rest of my meal in silence. I paid my tab and left the tavern.

The busy streets of London had died down slightly, the sun

had begun to drop, and darkness would arrive soon. I walked down the street, still not know where to go or look. I just walked straight down the road, watching people retreat into their homes before the light of day disappeared. I felt my muscles suddenly twitch and my head exploded with pain. I knew what was going to happen before it happened, another seizure. My vision began to become a tunnel with little light entering it. I jumped to the side of the road and into a living memory.

***

I looked all around the street I was on, and there wasn't a soul in sight, the air was eerily quiet. I heard something, a hum. It was faint, but still audible. It was London Bridge Is Falling Down, but it wasn't the usual cheerful tune. It sounded sinister, haunting. The song had all the power over me, I followed the tune to a dark alley. The shadows seemed to engulf the passage, but in the dark I saw someone, their dark hair shining in the dim light. "Faye!" I yelled. She ran away with incredible speed down the alley. I knew it was her, it had to be. I ran after her, the medicine bag hitting my side and the wind rushing across my face. As I ran through the alley the song became deafening, it was all I could hear. I ran as fast as I could, but around each corner of this seemingly never ending alleyway Faye seemed to be just out of reach. The music unnerved me as the deafening sound pierced my ears and captured me. I rounded the last corner, and reached the end of the alley. She was right in front of me. My eyes met hers and the music stopped. Day changed to night in the blink of an eye. I was here, with her. This is where we were last night, it felt as if I had just met her. We began walking. Faye looked at me. Her lips were moving but I couldn't make out a word. I assumed she was saying whatever we were talking about last night on this walk through the dark streets of London. I still could not make out a single building, or find any trace of life. We reached a house at the end of the road. No, not a house, an apartment. Faye looked at me. "Can I show you something?"she asked. I blinked profusely, shocked to hear her voice. I remembered the first time I had heard her speak, it had sounded so happy and full of life. This whisper, it sounded like an echo of that life.

"John?" she asked again.

"My apologies. What would you like to show me?" I asked nervously. She smiled and said "Follow me." She grabbed my hand suddenly, it felt as if ice had engulfed my body. She led me into the house. I was familiar with this place. It definitely wasn't a house, it was the apartment building. Her apartment building. As we entered, she led me through the main lobby to the edge of the room, beside the stairwell. But she didn't take me up the stairs to the room I woke up in. Instead she was staring at the tapestry that was beside the stairwell. She took down the tapestry, and revealed a door. I felt something, a sense of anxiety and dread that crept through my bones. I didn't know what was behind that door. I wasn't sure I wanted to know. Despite my hesitation, she swung the door open, and walked through the entrance with her back facing me. The mouth to the belly of the beast.

"You asked me what my occupation was earlier this evening, John. Would you like to know?" . I swallowed to keep from choking on the sandpaper that coated my throat.

"Why yes, I-" I started. I couldn't bear to finish my sentence. Faye turned around. What I was seeing in my eyes was not possible, not comprehensible. It was no longer Faye in the doorway, it was something terrible, something evil. The being had eyes that burned as if it were pure fire, skin that was ash gray. It looked almost human, but all I could smell was brimstone. The thing looked at me, and I came to the realization that this thing, this demon, resembled me. It smiled at me, revealing sharp teeth.

"Be careful what you wish for John" it smiled, stepping towards me. I froze, paralyzed by my fear. It came closer. The floor burned with every step. Fire rose up behind the demon, its grin never fading. Its face was right beside mine, and it hissed in my ear, "I know you are afraid, but you and I, we are the same. We will never be forgotten." The demon chuckled. It's hot, foul breath on my cheek was all I could feel. I couldn't move a single muscle. All I could do was listen. "Soon you will know everything, and soon, very soon, you will be reborn." It paused, I waited in anticipation. "But for now..." The demon moved away from my ear but stayed close. It raised its hand. It had long black talons, razor sharp at the tips so they were like daggers on its ashen hands. I wanted to move, but I couldn't. I was certain I was going to die, that this thing was going to gouge my eyes out, or something crueler. Instead it placed the palm of its hand on my face. That's when I awoke in the alley. Darkness had fallen, and I was alive.

I didn't know if what I had just experienced was a memory, or a nightmare. It all felt real, but there was no way to tell. I decided to return to Faye's apartment, I thought I would find my answers there. I felt relieved that I could walk with a purpose, with direction and stop being lost. I was able to pick myself up, my bruises brought me pain as I stood up. I picked up my medicine bag, and walked quickly through the streets, becoming a shadow in the dark hurtling towards my answers. I didn't know what time it was, all I knew was where I needed to go. There were lights that illuminated the streets, but all I could see was darkness. As I rushed through the streets, I wasn't seeing things clearly. Everything was a blur, a rush. I desperately needed to know just exactly what happened to Faye. Was there a demon that got to her? Was the demon even real? Was she safe? I needed to make this hell stop. So many questions rushing through my mind, all of which were interrupted by crashing into a lady. My senses were lost, no pain was felt, my vision was not processing anything or people that were in my way.

I snapped out of my intense trance when I crashed into a woman knocking both of us down, and her landing on top of me. "My apologies ma'am I-I-I didn't see you," I stammered. She replied breathlessly "Good heavens sir, my apologies. Are you alright?" I was surprised that she wasn't attacking me for bowling her over. "I'm alright, madam, my apologies." I said as I helped her up.

The pale light from the street lamp illuminated her face, it was hard to deny, and she was beautiful. Her hair was a light blond color, eyes blue like water of the ocean, skin a pale smooth white color, and her smile, it was beautiful. Just like Faye. "Faye…" I mumbled. "What did you say?" she asked innocently. "Oh, nothing. I just…Nothing. My apologies I must be going." I said quickly, with some shame that I had been staring at her for so long. She clearly noticed, and apparently didn't mind. "Oh! No, wait!" She grabbed my arm with surprising strength. Her eyes locked onto mine, she smiled sheepishly and asked "Could I walk with you? I don't like the dark and you seem like a strong man."

"Yes of course" I replied, stunningly quickly.

"Splendid, shall we?" she extended her arm. I was hesitant but I looped my arm around hers and we set out.

Why would an absolute stranger want to walk with me without even me knowing her name or her knowing mine. It was nice to have a companion to walk with, she seemed bubbly, intelligent, and she was beautiful. "Are you a doctor?" she asked, "Yes, how did you know?" I asked quizzically. "Your medicine bag" she giggled. I had completely forgotten that I had my medicine bag. We exchanged in more friendly conversation as we walked, until we reached the building. As we neared the apartment I began to feel cold, like something awful was about to happen. I looked at the dark windows of the building, it seemed like gateways to pure darkness, except for one, one window. On the window of the ground floor I could see something, it looked like the eyes of the demon. I froze, causing the woman I was with to jolt backwards "Oh my! What is wrong?" she exclaimed, I couldn't reply. There was nothing I could say, I couldn't say there was a demon, only a madman would say that. I couldn't be sure what it was. "Nothing" I replied nervously. "Well this is where I depart" I said quickly. Demon or no demon, I had to know where Faye was, I needed my answers. This ends now.

"Oh, but sir," the woman said, in a manner which meant something. She moved in close to me, and kissed me. I didn't know what to do, or why she was doing this. I didn't fight it, I allowed her to kiss me. The kiss was long, passionate. Before I knew what was happening the woman and I ended up in the apartment building, and entered Faye's room. It was a miracle we hadn't tripped going up the stairs. The door was still unlocked from the afternoon. I hadn't locked it. We still were kissing, and her hands began to lower. I felt as if I awoke at this moment, coming to the realization of what was going to occur if I allowed it. I didn't even know the woman's name. "Wait," I said, breathing heavily, out of breath from the passion and the raw emotion. "I don't even know your name, who are you?" I asked. She began to giggle and whispered in my ear "I am whoever you want me to be". I became suspicious, this wasn't how ladies acted, and proper ladies did not throw themselves at strangers.

I asked again with authority. "Who are you?". She must have realized that this was not a part of whatever game she believed she was playing. "We don't give out our real names, normally our clients make them for us." She said shyly. I knew what she was then. A prostitute. She almost got me, she almost made me...My thoughts halted as if a knife had been driven into my brain. Memories flooded me, almost taking me over. I knew what happened. I looked at the woman and said, "I normally let you decide your own name. Come with me. I have something to show you." I smiled at her. She smiled back replying "Call me Candice than". I nodded and beckoned Candice to come with me.

We went down the stairs, my medicine bag in one hand and the other clutching Candice tightly. We went to the bottom of the stairwell and arrived at the tapestry from my vision of the demon. I released Candice's hand and took down the tapestry, revealing the door. I opened the door, a gust of air breezing past my face. The musky scent of the cellar was prominent. "What's down there?" Candice asked curiously. I just smiled and gestured for her to descend the stairs. "Ladies first." She was smiling, but I could sense worry in her, she took a cautious first step, looking back at me once as if she was going to ask me something. Instead she made a second hesitant step. She froze on the stairs, and turned back again. She didn't notice what I had retrieved from the medicine bag. I pressed the chloroform soaked rag to her face. She didn't realize what happened. There was no fear on her face or realization what had happened. I caught her as she began to fall. She was light in my arms. I carried her down the stairs, cradling her gently.

I brought her to the cellar, the room was nearly empty. Darkness covered the room like a quiet lethal blanket, lit only by a dim candle that had lasted miraculously from the day prior. Cobwebs surrounded the perimeter of the room. Dust had covered the floor, making it look as if it was covered in snow, except for a single set of footprints. There was a few old broken chairs at the left side of the room, however the table in the middle of the room looked freshly dusted in the middle of the room with a mirror beside it, also freshly polished and cleaned. I followed the footprints, and set Candice down on the table.

The table was bare except for a lantern, I had clearly thought of everything, I picked the matches out of my medicine bag and lit the lantern. As I opened the medicine bag, and began to pull to tools I needed out and set them gingerly beside Candice's unmoving body. She was lying there peacefully, sleeping. She looked just like Faye did when she was lying there. I remembered when I met Faye and she had led me to her apartment, stripping down to her scandalous blue dress, trying to seduce me. I realized when Faye had tried to seduce me, same as when Candice tried to, they were sick. It was wrong for me to walk away from those suffering from this disease. I had to cure them, my mother killed my father because of this disease, and the scourge had to be eradicated. I took my syringe out of my medicine bag, it already had the solution in it. The effects of it was complete paralysis but the patient could still be awake, and feel everything. Pain was an essential part of the procedure, they had to feel the pain they cause others in order for the treatment to be effective. The procedure was not yet perfected but it would be, one day. I am determined to eradicate this scourge. I took the bone saw out of the medicine bag, I noticed Candice's eyes flutter open. The look of sheer terror could not be mistaken on her face, her eyes widened, her lips trembled ever so slightly as if she was trying to beg me to stop, to not do it. Just like Faye did.

***

I remembered my mistake with Faye, for a moment my

mind drifted off, and remembered that crucial mistake I made yesterday. I didn't administer the compound to Faye in time, she was able to wake up. Faye begged me, her pleading voice echoed in my head "please stop...No god! Please No!" she kicked out and hit my ribs. I fell down, Faye grabbed a chair with a broken leg and smashed it on my back. I was knocked back down to the ground. My adrenaline was high, I felt no pain. I have one purpose, to purge this evil. As Faye tried to run away I grabbed her ankle. She fell, I quickly crawled on top of her. I placed both of my hands on her throat, applying pressure. She struggled and fought. But it was no use, she eventually slipped into unconsciousness. I picked her up and administered the compound and began the procedure.

Candice fearfully stared at the bone saw, I felt the need to reassure her. "Don't worry, you're sick. But I'm here to help you." Sweat began to form on my brow, it was extremely hot in the cellar. I cut into her midsection, each cut going deeper and deeper. I had to fix her, I couldn't let what happened to me, my father, happen to anyone else. This scourge had to be eliminated, the world will be a better place without it. The procedure lasted moment , Candice began to go into shock, convulsing, her body was weak. Unable to take the pain. Faye lasted a little longer, but the result was the same. Death. It swooped in suddenly and claimed the souls of these women. When I killed them, like the bird I felt nothing, no remorse, no pity, and no mercy. I did my best to cure them, but some evil has to be purged. Not everyone can be saved. I wiped by brow with my bloody hands, breathing heavily, staring at Candice, just as I stared at Faye. "You are all the same" I said with disgust. "I tried to save you, but you just couldn't hold on, could you?" I almost expected the corpse to reply. I looked up at the mirror, and there it was, clear as day. The demon, it wasn't smiling, it wasn't moving. I didn't fear the demon anymore. I knew one thing for certain,

John Fallow is dead. Like a caterpillar becoming a butterfly, I am becoming something else, something beautiful.

I would perfect my technique, and I would eliminate the scourge plaguing this city, the world eventually. I decided to leave Candice's body out on the street for everyone to see, unlike Faye's, which I had hidden away. I couldn't remember where I had hidden Faye's body, but no one would ever know. I'm certain of that. I left the basement, dropped Candice's body by a brush outside of the apartment building, and returned to Faye's room. I washed the blood away from my hands. No blood had gotten on my clothes, thank god for that. I returned the tools to my medicine bag, placing each item in with care.

I went to Faye's bed and before laying down, got on my knees and began to pray, "Dear lord, I will act as your holy vessel, act in your good name, to rid the world of these atrocities. Thank you for giving me your blessings and purpose in life. Amen." I laid in bed smiling, for the first time in my life I had purpose, and I had meaning. I will not forget what I did, not this time, never again will I forget who I am. After I had killed Faye, I felt the pain from out scuffle and had administered too much painkillers which lead to my blackout and memory loss. I didn't need any painkillers tonight, my happiness overtook my pain. I looked up at the ceiling, and let my eyes slowly close quickly drifting off to sleep with a smile plastered onto my face.

I woke up at noon, hearing the loud commanding chimes of Big Ben, and I looked outside. I wanted to leave, it was too beautiful of a day to do otherwise. The sun was bright in the sky, with no clouds to obstruct its light. I walked out of Faye's room, closing it and locking it, this would be the last time I see this room.

As I walked down the stairs, I saw the last cop leave the apartment. Clearly someone had seen Candice's body and gotten the police. My smile got bigger, revealing my teeth.

There were no fingerprints, no clothes, and no murder weapon, nothing that could incriminate me, I made sure all of that disappeared before I went to sleep. I couldn't have anyone take me away from God's work.

I walked out the door and proceeded to walk to Winslow's bar. The walk took me about an hour, when I reached the bar word had spread about the murder, it was all I could hear. It even made the front page of the paper. One body found in the basement of the apartment, and another body found in the Thames. I guess they had found Faye. No suspects so far. I looked at the paper, and I found my name, my real name. The paper read 'Jack the Ripper At Large'. "Jack the Ripper," I whispered to myself. It felt right, it was who I truly was.

I was sitting at the bar and listening to Winslow talk to some of his friends. "Did you hear about the prostitutes found today? Slashed open, looked like they were dissected" He said shaking his head, "Poor girls, so many bad things in this town. Cops are swarming the town for this chap, hopefully this will scare him. Maybe this is the end of the killings?" Winslow said with some hope. Winslow looked at me and said "What do you think John?". I looked at him, my face unmoving, no emotion to be seen and replied coldly " No, I don't think this is the end" Winslow looked back towards his friends as if he didn't hear what I had said. My smile erupted. I looked straight ahead into the infinite nothingness, I felt a cold hand on my shoulder. It looked like pure ash. I heard it's words hiss into my ear "You have work to do Jack, they were only the beginning." I nodded my head in agreement. It was time to find my next patient.

BAD BARBER
NICK FORSTER

"Haircut?"

Rudolph Juniper frequented this barbershop for years and was familiar with its routines. He sat in the chrome and leather chair, not bothering to answer the obvious question. With a snap of the sheet, Jonah Slater covered the man; protecting his expensive suit.

The young barber took a deep breath, wishing the finicky customer had come in earlier when he was on break. He tucked tissue paper around Rudolph's neck. "What will it be today, Mr. Juniper? The usual?"

"Yes, the usual. Number one fade and side part. Exactly like it is now, just shorter."

His gruff undertone didn't help Jonah's temperament. He'd been working doubles all week and was exhausted. It was almost Christmas, and he was saving to buy his son Wondertron, the talking robot.

"It's a beautiful day today, isn't it sir?"

He thought conversation would ease the tension, but the man looked up, met the barber's eyes, and raised one eyebrow. Jonah took the hint. He liked a little small-talk to ease the awkward intimacy involved with cutting another man's hair, but at the end of the day, the customer was always right.

Besides, he'd heard it all before from Rudolph. He'd been in there for years: he knew all about how rich and successful he was, how well he looked after himself, how he didn't trust the banks. Some days the man was a veritable fountain of personal information. Today, he wanted silence.

Jonah glanced around the shop. It hadn't changed a lick since he first sat in these chairs as a kid: the chrome barber chairs, the waiting area, the tattered magazines, the hair on the tiled floor, the antique cash register, the smell of aftershave. The two rows of barber chairs faced each other with mirrored walls that fascinated him as a child: the spiralling reflections seemed to reach infinity.

He started with the fade. It was a delicate cut, starting from nothing at the neck and gradually reaching one inch in length by the top. The look was popular with the hipsters, but old Rudy had sported this look for years.

I wonder why his parents named him Rudolph? Did they like reindeer? I wonder if a reindeer would be a good pet...

"WHAT THE..."

Jonah's daydream was cut short by Mr. Juniper's cry. He looked down at the three-inch white stripe on the back of the man's head.

"YOU INCOMPETENT FOOL! What have you done?"

Jonah was flabbergasted. He dropped the clippers and put his hands up to his face. "Mr. Juniper, I'm so sorry!"

"Look what you've done to the back of my head. I look like an idiot!"

"I can fix it, sir. I can just make the fade a little shorter, so that..."

Rudoph wouldn't let him finish. "And be bald? You want me to be bald in the back. No, I will not be bald, I don't want to look like a moron."

There were several balding men in the shop at the time and they cast annoyed glances at Rudolph, who stood up, ripped the sheet from his neck and threw it to the floor. He stomped over to the coatrack and snatched his trench-coat from the hook.

"I want this man fired!" be bellowed. Gustav, the owner of the shop took up the apology.

"Mr Juniper, please. This one is on the house."

"If this man is not fired, then I will sue. I cannot look like this. Look what you've done to me."

Old Gus looked over at Jonah. "I'm sorry, son. But you have to go."

***

Jonah was devastated. Fired from his job right before Christmas. How would he buy the Wondertron now? They were 400 bucks. He grabbed his coat and went out the door to the parking lot, hot on the heels of Mr. Juniper. If only he could apologize again, plead for mercy, anything. Surely the man wasn't that cold.

Before he could catch up, he saw the Jaguar fire up and peel out of the lot. An idea struck him: follow him and plead for mercy on his doorstep. Jonah ran to his old beater, started it up, and followed Rudy out of the parking lot. Like a shadow, he followed the jag through the streets and into the rich part of town. Manicured lawns, ornate landscaping, and mcMansions lined the streets of the well-to-do.

He saw the car pull into a particularly large house on the corner. Rudolph got out, slammed the car door, and stormed into the house. Jonah parked on the street, plucked up his courage, and walked up the path to the entrance. Feeling smaller than the lawn jockey holding up the porch light, he raised his arm and knocked on the solid, oak door.

An eternity passed, and Jonah was about to knock again, when the door opened. Jonah shrank back as Rudolph opened the door, looking angrier than ever. He was wearing a red smoking jacket and had a glass of scotch in his hand. "What the hell are you doing here? Haven't you done enough?"

Jonah shuffled and looked down at his feet. "Um, Mr. Juniper, I just wanted to – "

Rudolph didn't let him finish: "How the Hell do you know where I live, anyway? Did you follow me?"

"Sir, if I may," Rudolph beseeched. "I'm so sorry about the haircut. If there's anything I can do, to, you know, make up for what I did... I, I need my job, sir, you see, I have a child...he wants a robot."

At this point, Jonah was practically begging, looking down at his feet, wringing his hands. He didn't notice the rich man put his drink down, and reach into his hall closet and grab his shotgun.

The sound of Rudolph cocking the shotgun – a sound Jonah had never heard in person – was one he'd known intimately from years of watching TV. Eyes wide open and hands up, Jonah took a step back, almost tripping down the step. Rudolph raised the gun menacingly. "You better get off my property, boy."

Jonah kept walking backwards. "I'm sorry, I'm leaving. I just wanted to say sorry."

"Get out of here you butcher, before I do to you what you did to my hair."

The barber turned and ran. He got in his car and screeched off, not believing what just happened. Did that maniac just pull a shotgun on me? Should I call the police?

***

Jonah tossed back another soda. He was so mad he could spit nails. He wanted a real drink, but he'd been down that road before. He had bigger responsibilities now: his son.

It would be tough to explain to Ernie how there'd be no presents under the tree. Furthermore, how would he explain having to go live with Uncle Sam next month when he couldn't pay the rent. Ernie loved Sam, but so much change can't be good for the little guy. Especially after what happened to his mom.

Jonah grasped the picture of his dead wife. It had been three years, but Jonah felt it like the wound had been torn open yesterday. His sweet, young wife; cut down in the prime of her life, with so much promise.

"Charlice, I'm glad you can't see me now."

He closed his eyes and hugged the frame. "I don't know how I messed it up so bad. When I had you, I had everything: the sun, the moon, the earth, more than diamonds and gold."

The word gold triggered something in his mind and he sat bolt upright. Gold.

I've got so much gold. Its's stashed away in my attic. I wouldn't trust the banks. Gold, you see, gold is the future.

That braggart Rudolph's voice echoed in his ears: the conversation he overheard in the barbershop just last week. *It's stashed away in my attic...*

"What a fool that greedy bastard is," Jonah muttered, a seed of a plan forming in his head. He would go to Mr. Juniper's house while he was out jogging. Another snippet of the braggart's voice re-played in the barber's brain: *Every night at seven o'clock I run five miles. It's the intelligent man that takes care of his body.*

He held his wife's picture up and spoke to it.

"I will take his gold. And then we'll see who the ignorant fool is! Gold, Charice. Then I can take care of our boy, and I won't have to cut hair for rich, ungrateful weasels anymore!"

The next day, Jonah put his plan into motion. Dressed all in black, he parked his car down the street from Rudolph's house and waited, like a gumshoe in one of those old movies. Sure enough, at seven pm sharp, Rudolph started out on his nightly run.

After waiting a couple of minutes, Jonah pulled his cap low over his face, got out and slipped between the houses. His heart beating like an un-levelled washing machine, he smashed in a basement window.

Passing the point of no return, he knocked in the shards of glass, climbed in, and ran across the basement to the stairs.

His heartbeat was beating so loud and fast, he probably wouldn't have heard the alarm even if it wasn't silent. He flew up the stairs to the second floor and found the attic hatch. It's then he saw the siren lights outside, the red and blue lights reflecting in the white hallway. *Oh no! What have I done?*

Jonah ran back the way he came and climbed out the window into the arms of the waiting police.

"Well, well. What do we have here?"

The cop looked almost happy to have caught the young lad so red-handed.

"Would you believe I'm the furnace repair man?"

"Get down on the ground and put your hands behind your head!"

***

Jonah paced the halls and climbed the walls. He'd never been in jail before. He was a barber, not a criminal. He was beside himself with worry and grief. Such a big consequence for such a momentary lapse in judgement. It had been a week and he was still in the cage. Awaiting trial, no one to pay his bail, and guilty until proven innocent. He was guilty, but that was beside the point.

He couldn't take much more of this. Being locked up was worse than he could ever imagine. Criminals were 'other' people, 'bad' people, not people like him. He'd been raised right by his momma and poppa. What was he doing, stealing? Jonah, lower than he'd ever been, got down on his knees and prayed. "Oh God, I'm so sorry I did what I did. I was such a fool."

Tears streamed down his face. He looked up to the heavens (in this case a concrete ceiling) and reached out for salvation. "Please. Please, get me out of here."

"What's that? You wanta to get out of here?"

Jonah did a double take. He didn't know that God had an Italian accent, but it made sense, what with the Pope and the Vatican and all being in Italy. "You wanta to get out of here?"

The second time he said it, Jonah realized the voice was not of God, but of the man next door, Vito Esperosi. Vito was about 6' 3" and 350 pounds. Apparently he was a mob boss of sorts. Close enough to God in here.

Jonah weighed his response carefully. "Um, yes I'd like to get out of here," he said, barely above a whisper.

"Talk to me. I'm a gonna tell you what your gonna do."

**

Jonah couldn't resist the offer Vito made him, in fact, he couldn't refuse. Ernie was with the CAS now, and not with the fishes, so Jonah did what he was told.

He was out, but he wasn't free. He'd be free when his task was over, Vito assured. But for now, he was on the business end of a sawed-off shotgun in First National Bank with the clientele on the floor, and the tellers filling his bag with cash.

He was covered in sweat, his nylon stocking squishing his

nose against his face, sopping wet. He scanned the nervous faces of the customers on the floor: a mom cashing a cheque, a plumber in for some petty cash, a waitress on her break, a business man.. *Oh my God, it's Rudoph Juniper. Please don't look up, please don't recognize me...*

Rudolph looked up. Instant recognition. "It's... It's you!"

Jonah took a step back.

"The guy who broke into my house! The thief! …. The barber!"

Rudolph, emblazoned, stood. He advanced on the nervous barber holding the gun.

"You son-of-a-bitch. The nerve. Everybody, this is a piece-of-shit barber who ruined my hair two weeks ago, then decided to rob my house. Now he's in here trying to steal our money."

"Take a step back, Rudolph. Get back on the floor!"

"Don't tell me what to do, barber"

"I mean it, Rudolph. Get down."

Rudolph took another step and Jonah pulled the trigger. Rudolph flew backward, the bullet blast knocking him off his feet and sending him flying, blood splattering everywhere.

Jonah grabbed the money from the scared teller and ran. The getaway car's engine revved like a lion and Jonah jumped in, fixated on the vile deed he just did. They sped through the downtown core and out through the suburbs. No one followed. He looked out the window and watched a man cutting his yard. Such a contrast between the freshly cut and the overgrown lawn….

"Hey! What the hell?"

Jonah looked down at the man bun that now lay on the floor that used to sit perched on the back of Junior's head. *Oh no, not again!*

Gustav grimaced. He put down his scissors and rubbed his head. "Jonah! You a daydream. You a such a bad barber!"

POETRY

THE DARK SPOT
WILLY PRIMEAU

1:

It starts with a feeling deep inside. It's all consuming at first. It takes control of everything that you recognize as being who you are. You don't know what to expect or how to take control or gain any sense of what to do or how to move forward. Everything that you are spasms in anguish for your next move. Everyday is a struggle to keep your composure as you just don't know where to turn. You cry inside as your sole shakes in anticipation of your next move. Can you do it? At times you feel like there just isn't enough of you to tackle life itself. You are afraid to make a move as you don't feel that you are strong enough inside. Do you have what it takes? Is there enough of what makes you the person that you are to make that first step forward? You shake in anticipation and live a life of anguish, denial and fear until you gather enough courage to take that first step forward. Then and only then will you be free of the turmoil that is you.

2:

You have it in your hand and you are unsure of what to do with it. Your brain hurts and you feel like you are going to throw up. You fight the urge to run and hide. After all it would be so much easier if you just gave up. You could just walk away and end it all right now. You could have ended your misery long ago. Maybe you just don't care enough to complete the task that you are longing to at least give it substance.

After all who would care or even know if you quit... but there is Something inside you that keeps on pushing you forward in an attempt to just get started. You pace... you sweat.... you cry.... you slap your face and scream out in anguish... but it is to no avail as nobody is listening and nobody can feel your pain.

You have tossed your weapon what seems like a million times but somewhere deep inside you you know that you have to push forward and complete the task that you have demanded of yourself. So after you muster enough courage you once again grab your weapon of choice and begin to write it down.

3.

I sit here frozen and unable to move. It is cold and dark yet in a way comforting. The darkness steals my breath away and traps me in its ever embracing arms. I am afraid yet I find great comfort in its solitude. I have been here so long that I have lost all sense of time and awareness. Just who am I anyway. I have been afraid and alone for so long that instead of fearing the darkness I now embrace its inclusiveness. After all it accepts me as I am... never judging... never shaming. I have been here so long trapped in this corner that I now call it home ... I am unaware of any other form of existence... But am I living... or am I trapped in a world of darkness, Fear and shame. Only I can make a change... Only I can wish for something better... only I can find the strength to escape the engulfing darkness that has become my cage. I have been here so long that I have become blinded by its power over me. I cry myself to sleep huddled in a ball of flesh and bone... surrounded by its penetrating power that is constantly stippling away my will to fight. I cry out in pain and anguish...pleading for someone to help me... but nobody is there in the shadows to reach out and save me.... nobody... nobody answers my call for help. Yet somewhere deep inside I begin to remember faint aspects of light that are part of my past ... that are also part of who I am or what I once was... Remembering the warmth and light of my past seems to help me... to make things not so dark... to give me hope and a new perspective of what I used to be... and might be once again. Inside me a light begins to grow and slowly yet ever so slowly warms the parts of me that have been frozen for ever so long. It seems like a lifetime... it seems like forever... but whenever I begin to accept the strength of the light.... Then and only then will I ever be able to step out of my corner... out of the darkness and finally be able to step into the light.

4.

I lost again. I never win. Why can't I stop. They say why bother. You never win. You are too big. You are too slow. Why do you bother? I keep trying but never win. I want to cry. I never win. I finished last yet once again. My feet are sore. My back just aches. The pressure on my lungs is insane. When will I ever finish this race. I challenge myself yet once again. When will it stop? When will it end? I have challenged myself over and over again. Yet isn't the challenge the thing that counts. The thing that makes everything worth it in the end. I make the choice yet once again. I step up to the line to start yet once again. I accept the challenge. I step up to the starting line and begin yet once again.

5.

The air is crisp. My hands are sweating. I feel like throwing up. I can feel the hair on the back of my neck stand on end. I am shaking. I can not move. I feel like time itself is frozen along side of me. I want to move but I hesitate in fear. Can I do it? Will I have the strength to follow through or at least attempt the task. I have tried in the past but have lacked the courage that is required to complete the task. I feel bad and a bit disoriented. Can I do it? Can I follow through? Oh God give me strength. Please give me the strength. I so need to follow through. Come on I can do this. I berate myself to try and ignite the fire that lays deep inside my sole. Come on Willy you got this? I don't know where I find the strength... but for some reason I manage to find the power that cleverly hides deep inside me to complete or at least make a challenged yet excitable attempt... and that is when... at this moment of a personal gut wrenching challenge... I lean forward for that first kiss.

POEMS
ETHAN SHANTIE

"fifth sun / tonatiu"

1.

in August I leave false skin and
turn toward bright sun on my pale
tongue.

2.

I am inhaling Phoenix and its alleyway graffiti;
becoming blacktop and traffic accidents .

3.

at night we sink into the springs of a pullout couch,
awake in morning to car alarm drug deals
echoing through dirt yards where we share cigarettes.

4.

by September we have collected Frida Kahlo postcards,
pregnancy dreams and the looming retreat
toward winter. our trip fleeting forever.

5.

sing your bastard latin and disappear
before we go. it is easier if we do not say goodbye.
i tell you i leave behind my second self and
take with me the sun

HUMAN SONGS AND TALL TALES
CHARLES LEGGETT

Bards

Benjamin Bagby: "bardic" solo performance of Beowulf; *with Ensemble Sequentia, the Icelandic "epic song theatre"* Edda, Viking Tales of Lust, Revenge and Family; *Perth Arts Festival, February 2002*

Edda opened with one old sibyl gliding
(with six breasts and a cone-shaped head) across the
stage who channeled Creation. Call me cretin—
I was *not* on the edge of any seat. And

yet, I *did* feel what Wystan Auden, playing
spirit guide to James Merrill in *The Changing
Light at Sandover*, tells of shading Merrill's
steps in Ephesus on a stroll through ruins:

I felt distinctly "*TIME LIKE A SCUDDING CLOUD
RACE...BACKWARD*," backward, offering pride of place
to all these human songs and tall tales.
Bagby was playing a harp with six strings

based on "remains of instruments" disinterred
from old Germanic burial sites. And if
fat Time declines to shut Its big mouth,
Bagby has learned how to floss Its fat teeth.

To a Woman Whose Online Dating Profile Says Her Very First Date, at Age 12, "went poorly" Because She Declined to Hold Hands

I did not know the lad well enough
To find out if his palms were as rough
    As the frightening puns
    That those Catholic nuns
Used for scaling the Devil's high bluff.

For Lena

Lorraine Hansberry's A Raisin in the Sun, *Seattle Repertory Theatre, October 2016*

The plant that made the journey made it well.
Hard journeys came before it, as we know.
It bears more love than anyone can tell.

Shielded, like a clam inside its shell,
And cradled in a woman's hands: we know
The plant that made the journey made it well.

To look at it, you'd think a field in Hell
Was where it was transplanted from, and so
It bears more love than anyone can tell

In its new home, where sunlight helps it swell
In green and vibrant health. When it tastes snow
This plant that made this journey and made it well

Will drink from Winter as if it were a well,
A darkling passage down to where roots grow.
It bears more love than anyone can tell

And sings of its survival like a bell
That through *our* darkling passages we follow.
The plant that made the journey made it well,
And bears more love than anyone can tell.

OBIT WRITER
MARK JACKLEY

OBIT WRITER

I give you
black words
in white space.

Maybe we go
to darkness,
maybe we go to light.

Maybe any words
will do.

SHE PUTS HER FACE ON AS SHE DRIVES

Wrinkles
branching like
December trees in wind

Arms open wide,
they grasp
nothing

Not the stars or birds—
birds
grasp them

5 POEMS
RUTH SABATH ROSENTHAL

Operation Safe Haven, July 1944

> "And you that shall cross from shore to shore
>   years hence are more to me,
>   and more in my meditations, than you might suppose."
>   Walt Whitman, *Crossing Brooklyn Ferry*

Thank God for you, *Henry Gibbins* —
your great hull filled with 874 of us
— Jewish brethren dark and fair,
tall and short, frail-boned and gaunt —
each of us a survivor reborn
in the wake of conscience.
Praised, our leaders, Ruth Gruber
and Captain Korn — and their leader,
Franklin D. Roosevelt.
And thank you, buoyant sea
revered for strong currents, changing tides,
gulls that glide the breeze,
assuage wounded spirit.
And bless you, fresh air that fills the ashen lungs

and sunken chests of those, like me,
who escaped a gas chamber and giant oven
and those who escaped
the gassing vans, then
being buried alive or dead
in a heap in a deep ditch.
Yes, thank God for you, *Henry Gibbins* —
your length of sky-crowned decks surrounded by
the trusted steel of your sea-speckled rail —
each measure of that a far cry
from barbed wire;
your dining hall filled with
foods and smells unfamiliar and wondrous,
enlivening the spirit, uplifting the soul;
the shelter of your stalwart bulk
during enemy bombardment —
its steel-hard halls, sleeping quarters
with tier upon tier of hammocks,
the warmth of blankets that cocoon us,
soft pillows that smother nightmares,
smooth withered souls; and beyond belief,
your glistening white toilets,
roll upon roll of toilet tissue.
Thank God for all this, especially for America —
land beyond my wildest dreams. Promised land
of the free, the brave and the lucky!

Longing

A longing for heart-quiet
in the inevitable fall
into Winter's short days of sun
forwarding to Spring's
longer days — a circling back
in the sameness of time.

Heart-and-mind-numbing time
with no respite. A longing to quiet
those thoughts playing back
battle after battle. The awful
repetition. Mind and life wasting.
And, in the darkest season,

the conviction that the sun
will only half-rise in this lifetime
of mine. Feeling that sting
as from a bee's disquiet
of green slumber. Swelling to a fault,
every damned day. Slamming me back,

season upon season. Holding me back.
Chilling me with doubt that sunshine
can overcome rainfall
and that, invariably, given time,
better times will come and quietly
advance into Spring. Fast forward, past Spring

to Summer, and onto Fall springing
back to Winter, and round again. Flashbacks
ever more glaring under the sun, then, quite
out of the blue — a glance, a nod. Overrun
with fluttering, my heart paces in time
with fledging love's free-fall.

And, with the passing of another Fall,
Winter heralds in the sweetest of Springs:
daffodils and Easter bonnets — a lifetime
of celebration ahead, no looking back.
Past risk and reason, I bask in the sun
that is love's shine. Rain or shine, quiet

in the peace of it all, Fall after Fall, back
to Winter, Spring, Summer. Quiet as a Spring sun
bursting through clouds. Love, for all time, requited.

Mothering Children

taking a long pregnant pause
after
i rush past
a white-haired mother
feeding her gray-haired son
in diapers & geri chair
my own mother
just down the hall
silent in diapers
& railed bed
the corners of her mouth
cradling dried hasty pudding
my turn to feed her
later
to check her face
her diaper
once again
to smooth her hair
smooth the bed sheets
sing her to sleep

Whitman, Incarnated

"I bequeath myself to the dirt to grow from the grass I
love, If you want me again, look for me under your boot-
soles."

Walt Whitman, "Leaves of Grass, Song of Myself"

Walt, it's over a century since you bequeathed us
your exuberance and optimism, your long trains of thought
on laborers and lovers, mother nature, human nature.

The century-old trees of your youth standing sky-high
in air fresh with optimism, now stand stalwart in airs rank
with intolerance, their limbs reaching upward

entreating heaven. I quake in the timbre of unrest
that surely would have waked you in a drench of sweat,
waves of foreboding. Foreboding that belies green —

the green of your luxuriant grass, the blush of your
autumnal hues, your snowflakes dancing upon bare branches
reaching far and wide, warming wanting hearts

and enlivening the earth with a melt giving way to
burgeoning spring. Earth, where today, flags raised,
nation after nation, shamelessly wave.

Oh Walt, if only you were here to unearth the green
of grass scorched in these flagrantly hostile days.
If only your inimitable ebullient praise of green

would serve to raise spirits worldwide; that your love
of mankind, your heart-warmed words proclaiming
that love, however translated, would be

the uncommon denominator among factions fractured.
Oh, that your humanity, translated into the yet unknown
territory of diplomacy, would then begin to close the breach

dividing the universal us.

From Wasteland to Heartland

I've got an especially niggling notion
to set my leaving machine in motion.
Too long having kept my tank full
of a slow-acting anti-vitriol
I'm finally leaving the swine who snuffed
out the light from my dreams. Enough!

Years of his perpetual two-timing
has my taut-as-wire smile past thinning
to the verge of snapping — wish
growing into *full-blown anguish*.
I can now see what defines *LaLa Land*
and unquestionably separates *Wasteland*

from *Heartland*. Even more revealing,
is how I can now relate to the universal saying
"landing on one's own feet." And so
I'm off this acreage of a weed-field — this
absolute wilderness where seeds sowed
reap only the most thankless of wishes.

And driving my trusty old tractor
24/7, I'm bent on finding a green pasture
ripe with only fruit of just reward
— one hell of a bloom'n orchard —
where, ever thankful that I'd stood
my ground, I will root myself for good.

NONFICTION

IN HER FOOTSTEPS
VICTORIA KLASSEN

They threw her! They *threw* the girl in the air. THREW.

My heart is pounding; my breathing, laboured. They want to do that to me too. They pick up the other girl in my group—the one with the high ponytail, dyed blonde hair, and pointy chin—and throw her into the air.

Holy shit. I can't do this. It doesn't matter though; it's my turn. The three girls stand together, intimidating in their height, age, and experience. They stare at me expectantly.

I take a deep breath.

I take a step towards them.

I remind myself why I'm here.

Before my mom was a CFL cheerleader, she was St. Mark Catholic High School's first graduating cheerleading captain. My aunt followed closely in her footsteps, and most recently my cousin Kyla was on St. Mark's cheer team. Now as a grade nine student, it's my turn. No pressure.

The cheerleading my mom and aunt did mainly involved dancing and pompoms. Today cheerleading is focused on stunting and gymnastics. Girls lift and throw each other into the air. They spin, flip, and fly.

The girl behind me grabs my waist and calls, "One, two." I

can't do this. I'm not a cheerleader, dancer, or a gymnast. I should go home. Instead, I shift my weight onto my tippy toes and jump into the two girls' waiting hands. Two of the girls—the bases who will lift me into the air—hold my feet at waist level while the third girl supports my bum.

The girl behind me yells, "Ready—one, two." They lift me up so my feet are now at their chest level. I'm standing before I know it, solid, as if it's second nature. My knees lock and every muscle in my body contracts. At my side, my hands tighten into fists; long nails dig into my palms. My first double base. The height is terrifying and exhilarating at the same time.

"Do you want to cradle?" calls one of the girls below me.

The fear returns, slithering its way back into my bones. They want to throw me into the air now. I press my lips tightly together, fighting an internal battle. I'm terrified and yet I desperately want to make the team. If I say no, I risk not making the first cut. Only 36 out of the 70 girls are going to make the team, and only nine of those girls will be tops—which is the position I'm trying out for.

My face must give me away because high-ponytail girl comments that I look scared. The girls holding me lower me to the ground. Once I'm back on the faded red mats I supress my frantic breaths. High-ponytail girl, with her beady eyes and insincere concern, tells me, "You should smile when you're in the air."

High-ponytail girl goes up in a double base and begins making ridiculous faces in the air. She winks, nods, and opens her mouth like a gaping fish. I wonder where her smile is.

A petite woman stops by, a clipboard in her hands. Mrs. Mahar is the school's cheerleading coach and upper year math teacher. I'm unaccustomed to feeling tall, being only five feet, but my arms suddenly feel awkwardly long as I look down to greet her. She asks me if I'm Kyla's cousin.

"I was Kyla's coach for six years," says Mrs. Mahar, her voice warm and welcoming. "It's nice to meet you."

With the coach watching, it's my turn again. I supress my fears, get back into the air, and let them cradle me. They throw me into the air and after one second of weightless free flight, the three girls catch me. Their strong arms securely grasp my back and legs while I stay tight in a plank position, facing the sky. My body is buzzing with adrenaline and a real smile forms on my lips.

The three tryouts morph into four, then five, then six—turning into three long and agonizing weeks. With every passing tryout, I want to make the team more and more.

The final list is posted while I'm in class. Lidia, another girl trying out for the team, sits beside me. We look at each other with excited dread.

"You can go check the list," I say. Lidia had confided in me earlier that she wouldn't be able to handle someone else telling her she didn't make the team. She disappears through the doorway.

Tick.

Tick.

Tick.

Finally, Lidia returns and sits down.

"I made it!" she shrieks.

"Congrats!" I give Lidia a hug as she bounces up and down.

"How about me?" I dare to ask.

"Well, you see, I wasn't finished looking at the list and I heard someone coming...so I left because I didn't want to get in trouble," Lidia replies.

I stare at her, "Seriously?" I can't decide if she's lying.

Raising my hand, I ask the teacher for the bathroom pass.

As I walk down the hallway, anxiety is already weaselling its way into every niche in my body. My chest is constricting, becoming heavier with each step. I know I didn't make the team. Lidia just didn't have the courage to tell me. She knows how much this means to me. I want to be happy for her, but bitterness prevents it. It's unfair that she made the team when I'm the one who wants this more then she could ever understand. My steps echo in the vacant hallway. With each stride towards the gym, I accept the fact that I haven't made the team. It's disappointing to make it to the last tryout, just to be cut. How am I going to tell my mom? It isn't even just about my mom anymore. It's about me now. I want this.

I arrive at the list and scan it. Sure enough, there is Lidia's name, high-ponytail girl also made it, and then—

Victoria Klassen

The second name from the bottom stares at me. I gape at it, eyes wide. My disappointment disintegrates, replaced with bubbles of weightless joy working their way up my chest. I double-check the list and head back to class. I float down the hallway my mother once walked.

I pull out my cellphone, "Mom, I made it!"

ABOUT THE AUTHORS

Nicholas Forster is a builder of both time and space, crafting homes by day and stories by night. He is the author of such short stories as "Asteroid Adventure", "Ordinary Oliver", and "The Toad". He hopes to complete the A-Z anthology one day; but for now, he is polishing up his first novel and thinking about the next. Nick hopes to journey beyond the work-a-day world of home construction and create his own collected works. His stories explore themes of adventure and heroism, and the possibilities of the human spirit. As Gandalf once said, "We have to decide what to do with the time that is given us," and Nick decides to write.

Jason D. Grunn can't get enough of stories. He thinks about them, reads about them, watches them, imagines them, writes about them, and in a way, is them. As the Persian Poet Rumi once wrote, "When you do something from your soul, you feel a river moving in you, a joy." The river, the soul, is his source. His passion, writing, is his conduit to it.

Mark Jackley's work has appeared in *Fifth Wednesday*, *Sugar House Review*, *Natural Bridge* and other journals. His newest book of poems is titled *On the Edge of a Very Small Town*.

Natasha Kirmse is a current student of Carleton University's English and Film programs. Her passion for the English language and the worlds it can create through fiction have guided her interests both personally and academically throughout her life. Natasha's other published works include children's book *Sam's Shadow*, and her more recent novel *100 Ways to See the World*.

Victoria Klassen founded Carleton University's Book Ravens club while studying journalism and English, and went on to pursue her Masters in Communications. She can be found writing about mermaids but refusing to swim in cold water, drinking tea after a long day of skiing, or buying more books than she can possibly read.

Charles Leggett is a professional actor based in Seattle, WA, USA. His poetry has been published in over three dozen journals in the US, the UK, Ireland, Australia, New Zealand and Canada (*Scarlet Leaf Review*, Toronto), and has twice been nominated for the *Pushcart Prize*. His long poem "Premature Tombeau for John Ashbery" was an e-chapbook in the Barnwood Press "Great Find" series.

Jennifer Ng is a writer in San Francisco. She recently published a nonfiction book, *Ice Cream Travel Guide*, and is working on a novel based on her grandparents' lives in China, Peru, and the United States. Her work has appeared in *Arkana*, *Cold Creek Review*, and *Airplane Reading*. In her writing, she explores identity and relationships. If she was asked about her favorite hobby at the age of 8, she would have answered "observing", which is still a joy and an inspiration for storytelling. Read more of her work at jennism.com or follow her on twitter: @jennism.

Brice Peters is a Carleton University honours student with a major in neuroscience and a minor in chemistry. Brice is passionate about writing and this is his first time being published. Brice is a part of the ACACIA fraternity and lives in Ottawa.

Willy Primeau has a worldly experience in acting, singing, dancing, and in many different forms of creative and expressive writing. He started writing at an early age while in high school, where he wrote a short one person act titled "A Fathers Covenant". He has worked with groups of people in expressive writing and art. He is the proud father of four amazing and creative children and five wonderful grandchildren. He has been married to an amazing woman for thirty-six years.

Ruth Sabath Rosenthal is a New York poet, well published in the U.S. and, also, internationally. In October 2006, her poem "on yet another birthday" was nominated for a *Pushcart Prize* by Ibbetson Street Press. Ruth has authored five books: *Facing Home – Facing Home and beyond – little, but by no means small – Food: Nature vs Nurture* and *Gone, but Not Easily Forgotten*. The books can be purchased from Amazon or directly from Ruth, via her website: newyorkcitypoet.com. Her other websites are poetrybyruthsabathrosenthal.com and bigapplepoet.com.

Terry Sanville lives in San Luis Obispo, California with his artist-poet wife (his in-house editor) and two plump cats (his in-house critics). He writes full time, producing short stories, essays, poems, and novels. Since 2005, his short stories have been accepted by more than 280 literary and commercial journals, magazines, and anthologies including *The Potomac Review, The Bitter Oleander, Shenandoah*, and *The Saturday Evening Post*. He was nominated twice for *Pushcart Prizes* and once for inclusion in *Best of the Net* anthology. Terry is a retired urban planner and an accomplished jazz and blues guitarist – who once played with a symphony orchestra backing up jazz legend George Shearing.

Ethan Shantie is a graduate of the SUNY Potsdam Creative Writing Program where he studied under the Mohawk poet Dr. Maurice Kenny. He has previously published two books, *Poems for Danielle Steel's Purple Prose* (Many Moons Press) and *we meet by accident* (Ghost City Press). His band Sunflo'er is set to release their second LP in Summer 2018. More of his writing and collage work can be found on Instagram @ethanshantie.

Mary Sword is a fourth year English student at Carleton University. When not writing Mary can be found working in the theatre, both on and off stage, within Ottawa. Writing is one of her passions and she is so happy to have had the opportunity to write for this anthology. She'd like to thank the editors for all their hard work.

George Talin lives in Ottawa, Canada. Passionate about worldbuilding, he writes short stories framed in his magical world of Mezion. His science fiction stories are woven into a tapestry of many different worlds, known and unknown, from plausible to fantastical. His goal is to create worlds that you lose yourself in. From short stories offering interesting tales, to rich lore, unique characters, and world-changing moments, he hopes to take you on a journey through worlds.

Nathaniel Neil Whelan is a trained historian and up-and-coming author. He has a Master's degree in European, Russian, and Eurasian Studies from Carleton University and is currently enrolled at Algonquin College for Professional Writing. When he's not writing, Nathaniel is hard at work turning his apartment into a Funko POP! museum. He lives in Ottawa with his partner and pet cat Susie-Bear.

Laura Wilson was born in Belfast, Northern Ireland and moved to Ottawa with her family when she was nine. She studied accounting at the University of Ottawa and then went on to obtain her accounting designation and started working at Carleton University. She is now following her passion for reading and writing by studying part-time at Carleton in the hopes of obtaining a Bachelor of Arts in English with a specialization in Creative Writing. She is also working on a novel and dreams of filling her days with words instead of numbers.

ABOUT THE EDITORS

Nathan Primeau majors in English and minors in film studies at Carleton University. His work has appeared in three DeeBee Publishing anthologies, Cult Mag, and the now-defunct Anthem Little Magazine. Nathan lives in Ottawa, with his partner and their two silly dogs.

Abigail Rabishaw is an English major at Carleton University. Her work has appeared in two DeeBee Publishing Anthologies, and she has previously edited for Typehouse Literary Magazine. You can find her on social media as @abbyrabishaw. She lives in Ottawa with her partner (who is also her co-editor) and their two dogs.

DEDICATION

This book is dedicated to all the patient contributors included within that waited as we pushed through this long and harrowing journey into publication. Thank you.